JOLLY
& JADED

JOLLY
& JADED

INTERNATIONAL BESTSELLING AUTHOR
DJ KRIMMER

Cover Designer : SOREN DESIGNS
Formatter: DJ KRIMMER

Dedication

To those who find magic in the twinkle of lights, warmth in the glow of a fire, and joy in the simple act of giving.

This book is for you.

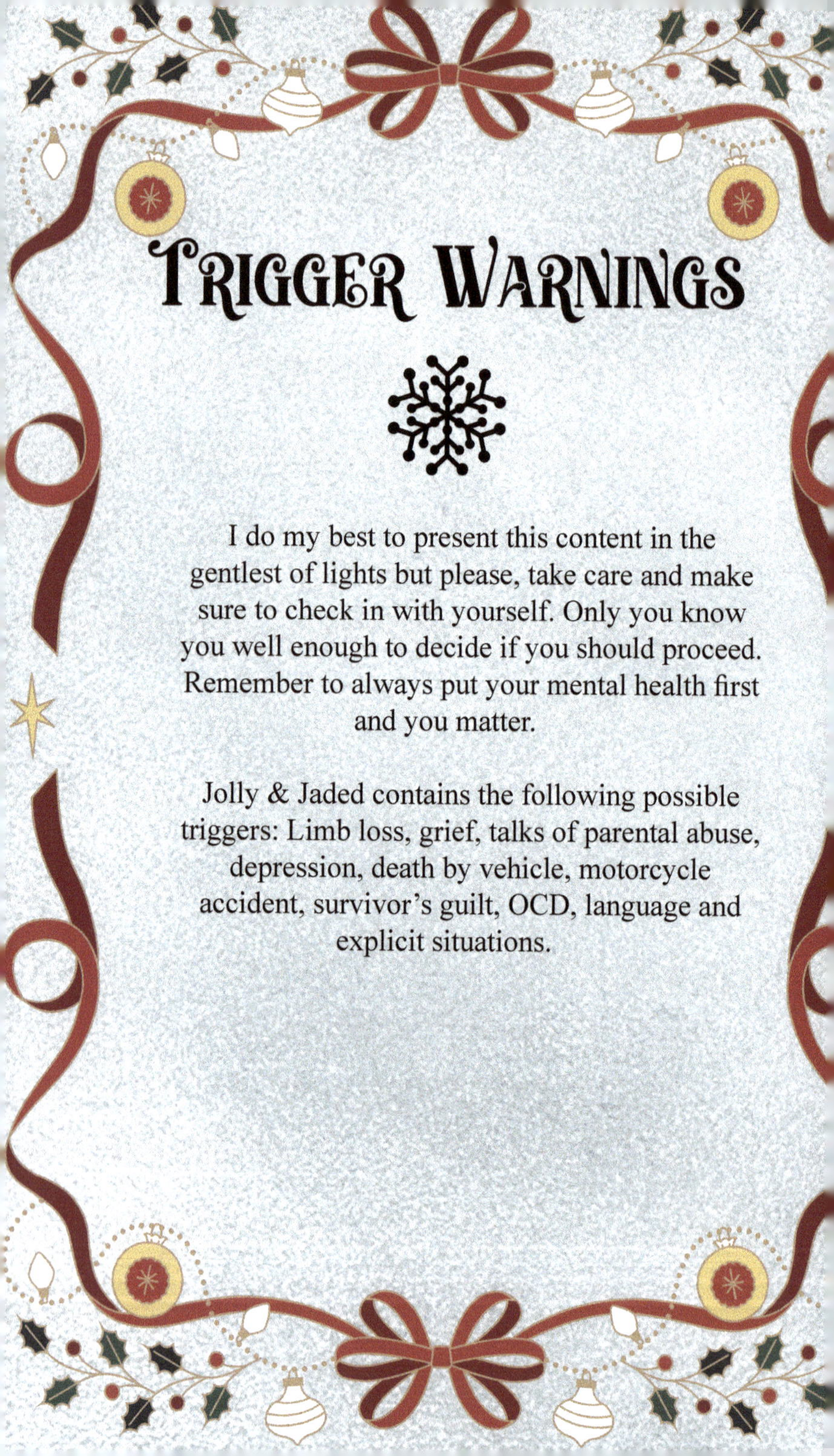

Trigger Warnings

I do my best to present this content in the gentlest of lights but please, take care and make sure to check in with yourself. Only you know you well enough to decide if you should proceed. Remember to always put your mental health first and you matter.

Jolly & Jaded contains the following possible triggers: Limb loss, grief, talks of parental abuse, depression, death by vehicle, motorcycle accident, survivor's guilt, OCD, language and explicit situations.

Playlist

Have Yourself A Merry Little Christmas — Sam Smith
Meet Me At The Mistletoe — Dave Barnes
My Santa Claus — Jessie James Decker
Under the Weather — Chris Young
All I Want for Christmas Is You — Michael Bublé
Under the Christmas Lights — Gwen Stefani

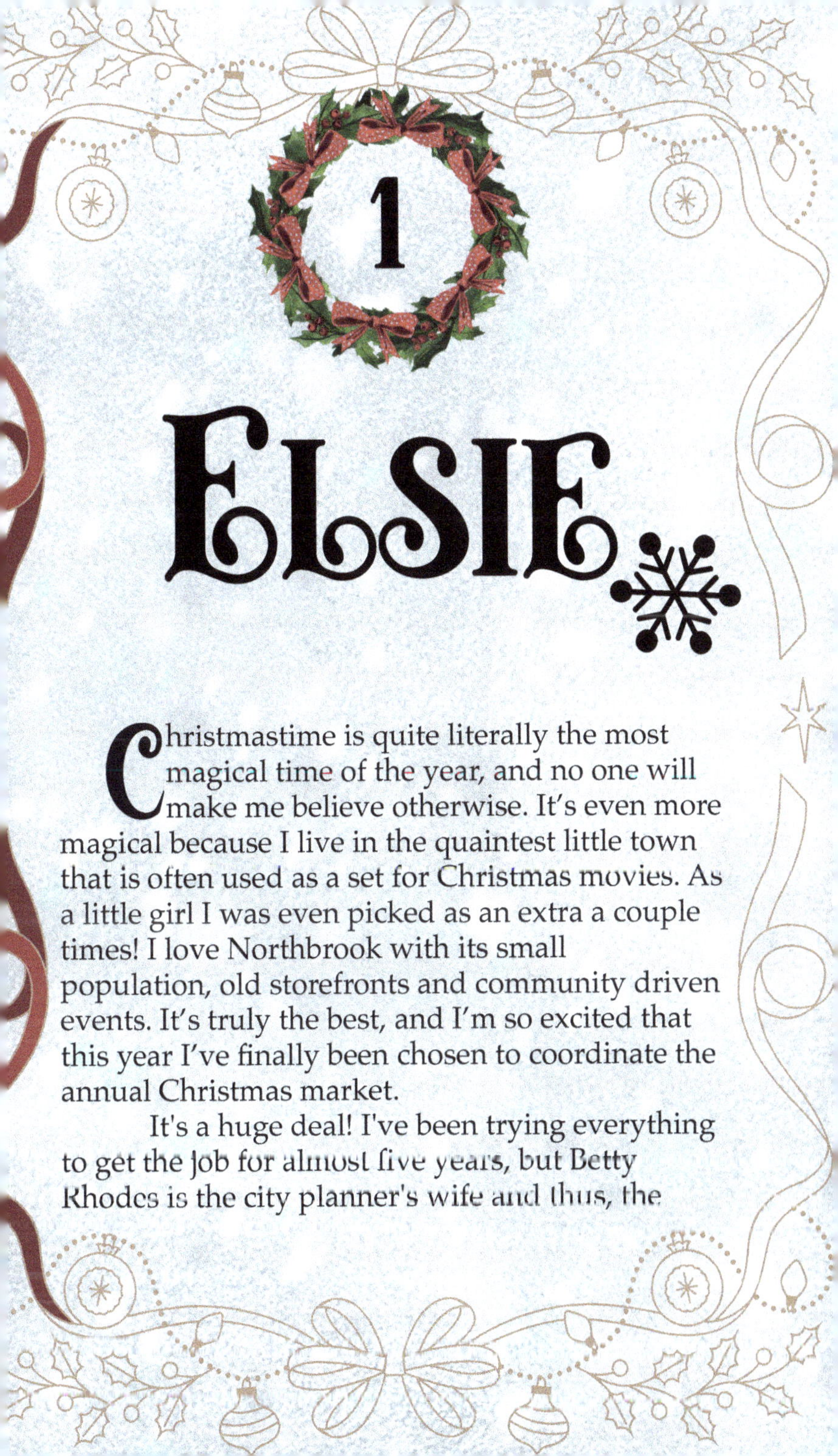

1

ELSIE

Christmastime is quite literally the most magical time of the year, and no one will make me believe otherwise. It's even more magical because I live in the quaintest little town that is often used as a set for Christmas movies. As a little girl I was even picked as an extra a couple times! I love Northbrook with its small population, old storefronts and community driven events. It's truly the best, and I'm so excited that this year I've finally been chosen to coordinate the annual Christmas market.

It's a huge deal! I've been trying everything to get the job for almost five years, but Betty Rhodes is the city planner's wife and thus, the coveted job always falls to her—except this year. This year, Betty fell down the stairs at the community arts center and broke her hip. I'm not happy about her injuring herself, despite the smile I currently have on my face. I would never want someone to get hurt but, if I were to enjoy seeing someone get knocked down a peg, it's Betty Rhodes. The woman allows her very minuscule power to go straight to her head. She uses the Christmas market as a popularity contest. All year the vendors will kiss her butt in order to get preferred spots and it's not fair! The market used to be a place where Santa would sit for pictures and there would be crafts for the kids and lights and an ice sculpting contest. Now it's scented candles and over priced jewelry, and children—while not banned—are not exactly welcome. But not this year, this year I'm bringing Christmas fun back to the market.

"Next!" I call from my place behind the counter at *Not Your Average Joe* – my coffee shop. I love this little shop. It was once a bookshop run by my grandmother but she outgrew the space after a social media influencer came by and showed off her rather extensive dark romance selection. After that— *Spines and Vines* became a hotspot for all the romance loving readers and she had to move to the corner building next store—leaving me to run the coffee shop.

Looking up from putting the peppermint mocha muffins in the case, I come face to… chest with Grant Anders. Grant the Grump as he's known—by only me. No one else would look at this intimidating man and dare give him a nickname of any sort. But I've known him since we were kids. I lived through him during his awkward teens and his voice change—he can't intimidate me. And I wouldn't call him that if he wasn't always so scowly; and then there's his muttering and grunts. I keep telling him, 'Grunts aren't greetings'. He hates when I say that—so obviously, I can't help but say it any chance I'm given.

"Happy Hump Day, Grant!" I sing out while beaming brightly. The way-too-attractive, black-haired man grimaces at my overly cheery greeting—which, why come in here twice a day when you know I'm going to annoy you?

"It's Wednesday," he grumbles out, and his overly annoyed attitude causes me to giggle.

"Obviously! Wednesday means we're over the hump of the work week! Thus, hump day."

"I'm going to have to ask you to stop saying 'hump'," he states while looking around the shop. For what, I don't know. I'm the only one who works here and nothing has changed since he was in here last night before I closed.

"Can I just get a large black coffee, please."

"Oh come on, Grant! I just got some new blends in this morning and some delicious holiday flavors!" Reaching into the case I pull out a tray of pastries. "How about a sugar plum danish?"

"Elsie." His sigh is tired and one of annoyance. It's one I'm very used to. He's been giving me that same sigh for years, especially

since he and I stopped hanging out. It's not that we were besties or anything, but my big brother, David and Grant were best friends growing up, so because I was the outcast—still am—I always tagged along in their adventures, like the three musketeers!

...or like a third wheel—whichever.

But since my brother's passing about six years ago, Grant has pulled away. He's become this closed off grouch and acts as though I am a nuisance to him, despite him coming in here constantly. Like, make your own coffee at home if I annoy you this much.

"Okay." I give him a tight smile, feeling somewhat discouraged. It's not just him, most are not into my coffee shop unless they are here for the bookstore. They come in, ask for a large black coffee and then scoff at the price and leave. "Large black coffee, coming up." I turn to grab the most festive of the Christmas themed cups to pour his coffee in—Rudolph, perfect.

"Did you hear I'm in charge of the Christmas market this year?" I ask, turning back around. "I'm hoping to make it like the old days when we were kids! Remember? With Santa and all the festivities for the families?"

"Perfect," he mutters, handing me a ten dollar bill. "Can't wait for that loud-ass crowd." He turns to walk away as I call out to him.

"What about your change?"

"Keep it," he calls out as the door shuts behind him.

"You bothering Grant again?" I jump at my grandmother's voice as she walks in from the back. I beam brightly at the small, older and heavily tattooed woman. I'm small but my grandmother is under five feet for sure. Though she has the attitude of someone two feet taller. I love her so much and firmly believe that I'm only alive today because of her.

Her grey hair goes down to her mid back and is in a thick braid that swings as she walks toward me, leaning on her cane. She beams while winking her wrinkled eye that has a tiny heart tattoo at the corner. "When are you going to make your move? I ain't gonna live forever."

"Oh please, you'll outlive us all. Besides—" I feel my cheeks heat as I hold the ten dollar bill in my hand. Everyday, twice a day Grant pays ten dollars for his two dollars coffee. "You know he doesn't like me."

"Ah," she scoffs before walking behind the counter to grab a coffee. "You're gonna have to stop being so shy if you want in his pants, kiddo."

"Anyone ever tell you you're very vulgar for a grandmother?" I joke as she waves me off. Though I do agree with her. I've had a crush on the guy since we were teens. And I've spent the better part of my life trying to get him to notice me, which I've failed at in every way possible—short of me breaking into his house and laying naked, spread eagle on his bed. Even still, he'd avert his pretty blue eyes and grumble something about getting me a shirt. It's so frustrating, because I know if I could just get him to really talk to me, he'd realize that we would actually get along really well. But he won't. It would take way more than a Christmas miracle to get Grumpy Grant to look at me.

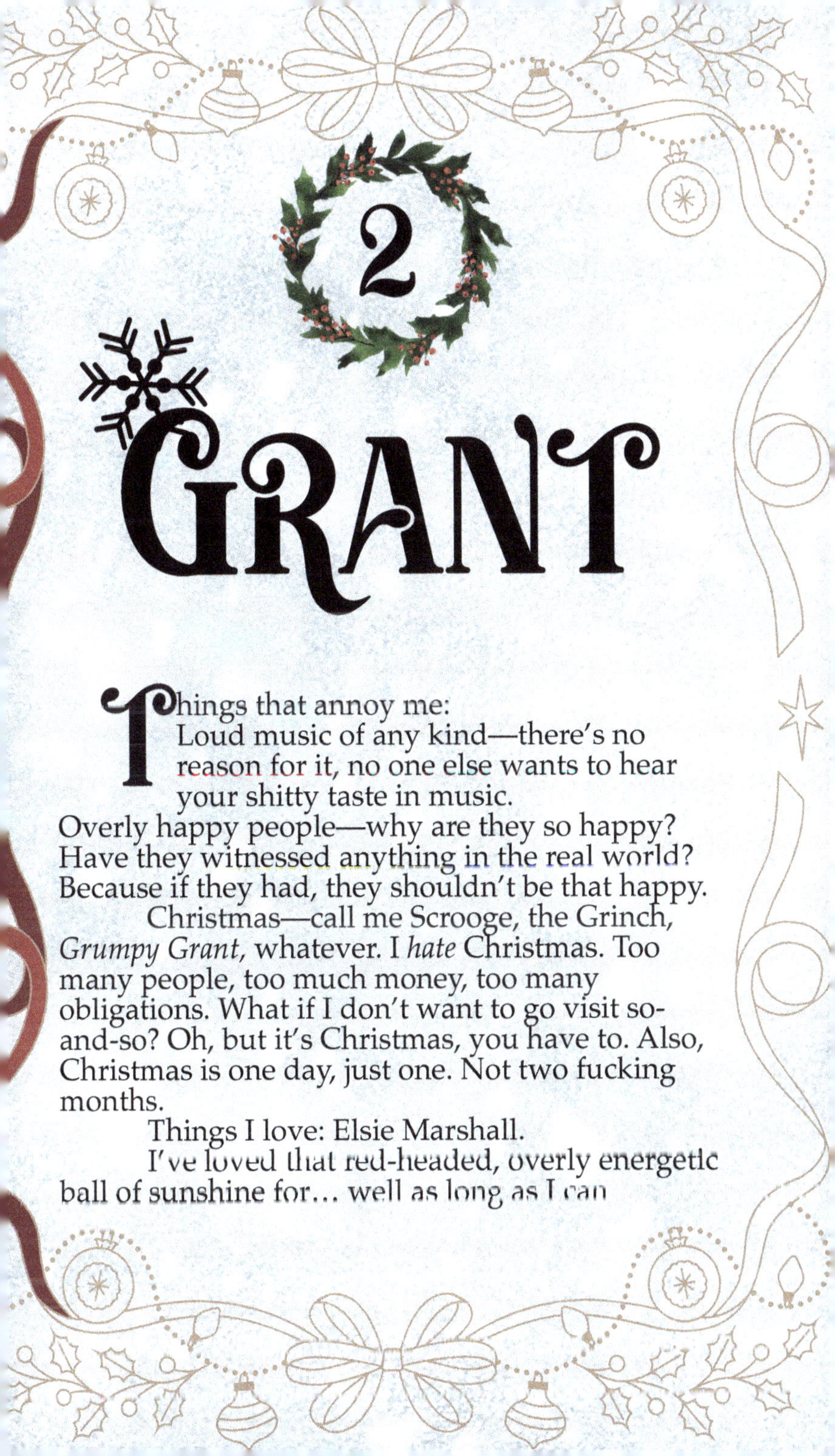

2

GRANT

Things that annoy me:
Loud music of any kind—there's no reason for it, no one else wants to hear your shitty taste in music.

Overly happy people—why are they so happy? Have they witnessed anything in the real world? Because if they had, they shouldn't be that happy.

Christmas—call me Scrooge, the Grinch, *Grumpy Grant*, whatever. I *hate* Christmas. Too many people, too much money, too many obligations. What if I don't want to go visit so-and-so? Oh, but it's Christmas, you have to. Also, Christmas is one day, just one. Not two fucking months.

Things I love: Elsie Marshall.

I've loved that red-headed, overly energetic ball of sunshine for… well as long as I can

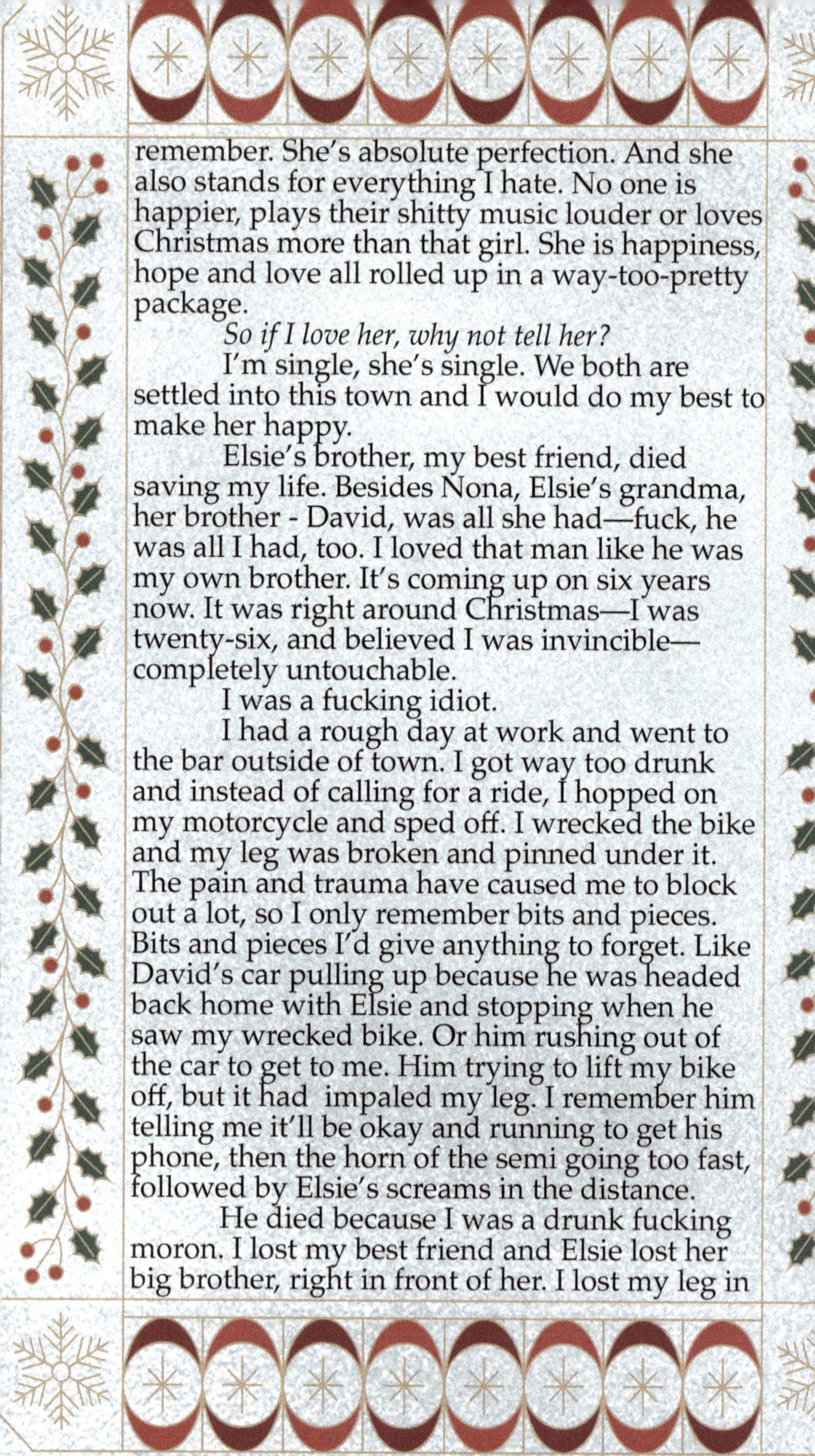

remember. She's absolute perfection. And she also stands for everything I hate. No one is happier, plays their shitty music louder or loves Christmas more than that girl. She is happiness, hope and love all rolled up in a way-too-pretty package.

So if I love her, why not tell her?

I'm single, she's single. We both are settled into this town and I would do my best to make her happy.

Elsie's brother, my best friend, died saving my life. Besides Nona, Elsie's grandma, her brother - David, was all she had—fuck, he was all I had, too. I loved that man like he was my own brother. It's coming up on six years now. It was right around Christmas—I was twenty-six, and believed I was invincible—completely untouchable.

I was a fucking idiot.

I had a rough day at work and went to the bar outside of town. I got way too drunk and instead of calling for a ride, I hopped on my motorcycle and sped off. I wrecked the bike and my leg was broken and pinned under it. The pain and trauma have caused me to block out a lot, so I only remember bits and pieces. Bits and pieces I'd give anything to forget. Like David's car pulling up because he was headed back home with Elsie and stopping when he saw my wrecked bike. Or him rushing out of the car to get to me. Him trying to lift my bike off, but it had impaled my leg. I remember him telling me it'll be okay and running to get his phone, then the horn of the semi going too fast, followed by Elsie's screams in the distance.

He died because I was a drunk fucking moron. I lost my best friend and Elsie lost her big brother, right in front of her. I lost my leg in the accident. They had to amputate my right one above the knee and now I walk on a prosthetic. I should've died. I would gladly throw my life down if it meant Elsie and Nona could have David back.

I've spent these past six years doing everything in my power to take care of Elsie— but only from afar. I rarely spoke to her after that night, except to shout at her when I woke up in recovery. I didn't mean to, but I was so full of grief and regret. Plus the surgeries and medications I was on didn't help. And she was there. She was there, with her grey complexion, dull, red-rimmed eyes, and a scowl I'd never seen on her before. She was there during the worst time in her life and she was caring for me. I lost it. I lost it because I didn't deserve her kindness. So I screamed until she left. It was months before I had the balls to see her again. How could I? She was twenty and I took her brother. How was I to ever look her in the eye again?

About two years ago, I was working for the town on a construction job with a few of my men, and every day for a month, Elsie would walk to our job site with coffee and pastries from the coffee counter at Nona's bookstore, while flashing her high-wattage smile. God that smile. I'm convinced her smile could bring about world peace if shown to the world leaders. Elsie's a firm believer that everyone is capable of being her best friend if they just got to know her. And she's right, they would be. But it's not for the sweet reasons she thinks. It's because people are mostly shit and love to prey on those who have a big heart and generous personality. Which is why Elsie runs

a successful coffee shop but has to live in the back of it.

Need money? Tell your story to Elsie.

Need food? Ask Elsie.

It's fucking infuriating. I have watched that girl give money to people who didn't need it and then go without actual food. And like I said, now she's living in the break room at her shop in secret. Because when the city finds out, they will make her leave.

I'm constantly trying to find ways to sneak money to her. Whether it be through tips, Nona, or in one desperate attempt, I told her that I was moving shit at my place and found money that David had stashed there as savings. Elsie believed me and graciously took it because she was about to lose the coffee shop due to loaning money to an ex that "swears he's good for it".

I adore the woman, but it's becoming increasingly more difficult to protect her from afar. And now she's doing this fucking Christmas market thing. This will be what ruins her. The people involved will bleed her dry of not only her resources, but her joy. She's a chronic people pleaser and I'm supposed to expect that she'll be able to handle the bitching of the vendors who fight her over the "prime spots"?

No, absolutely not.

"I charge a viewing fee." I jump and nearly spill my coffee as Nona's heavily tattooed, tiny body seems to materialize in front of me.

"Fucking Christ, Nona," I hiss while setting the book back on the shelf. "You trying to give me a heart attack?"

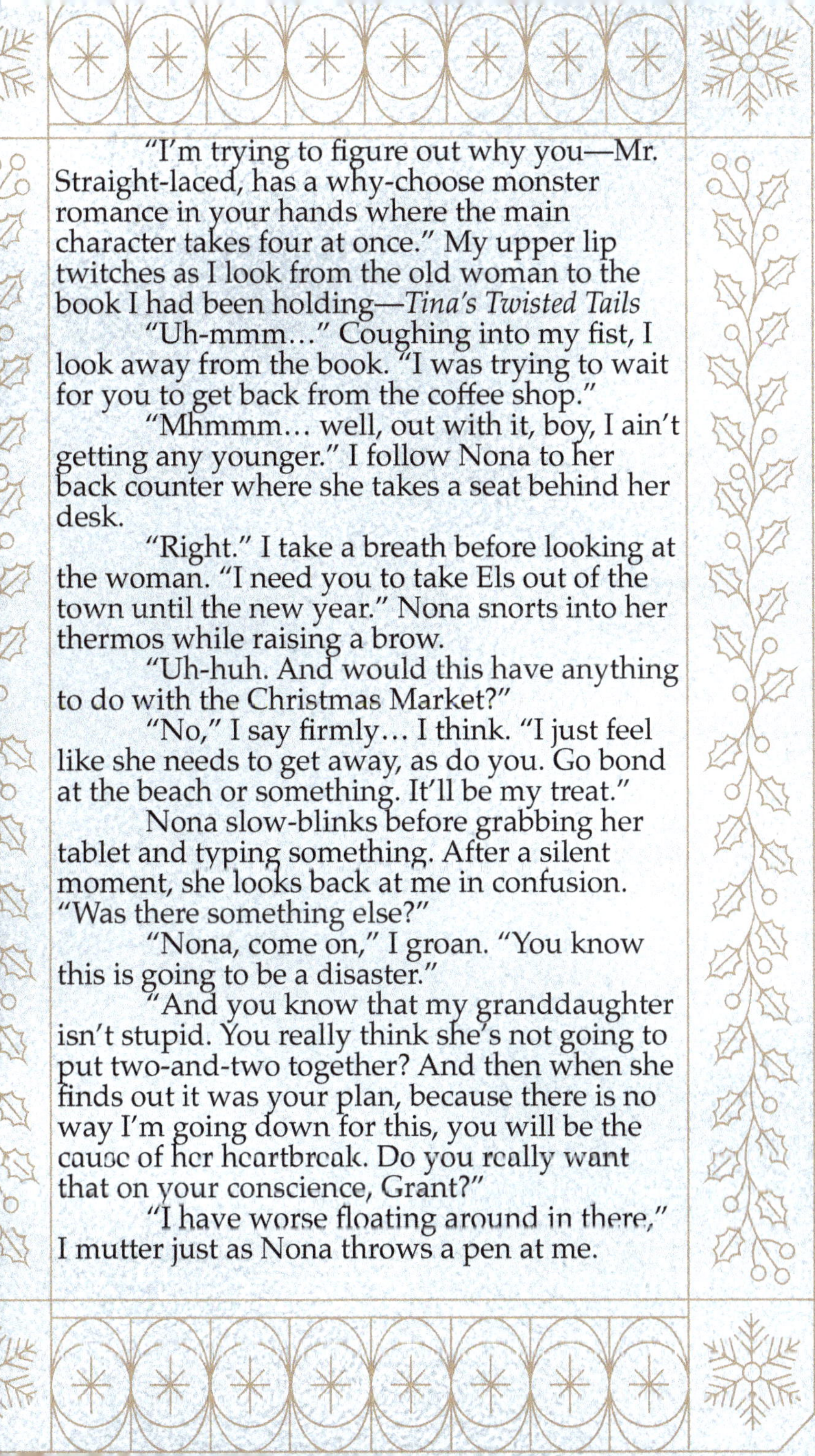

"I'm trying to figure out why you—Mr. Straight-laced, has a why-choose monster romance in your hands where the main character takes four at once." My upper lip twitches as I look from the old woman to the book I had been holding—*Tina's Twisted Tails*

"Uh-mmm…" Coughing into my fist, I look away from the book. "I was trying to wait for you to get back from the coffee shop."

"Mhmmm… well, out with it, boy, I ain't getting any younger." I follow Nona to her back counter where she takes a seat behind her desk.

"Right." I take a breath before looking at the woman. "I need you to take Els out of the town until the new year." Nona snorts into her thermos while raising a brow.

"Uh-huh. And would this have anything to do with the Christmas Market?"

"No," I say firmly… I think. "I just feel like she needs to get away, as do you. Go bond at the beach or something. It'll be my treat."

Nona slow-blinks before grabbing her tablet and typing something. After a silent moment, she looks back at me in confusion. "Was there something else?"

"Nona, come on," I groan. "You know this is going to be a disaster."

"And you know that my granddaughter isn't stupid. You really think she's not going to put two-and-two together? And then when she finds out it was your plan, because there is no way I'm going down for this, you will be the cause of her heartbreak. Do you really want that on your conscience, Grant?"

"I have worse floating around in there," I mutter just as Nona throws a pen at me.

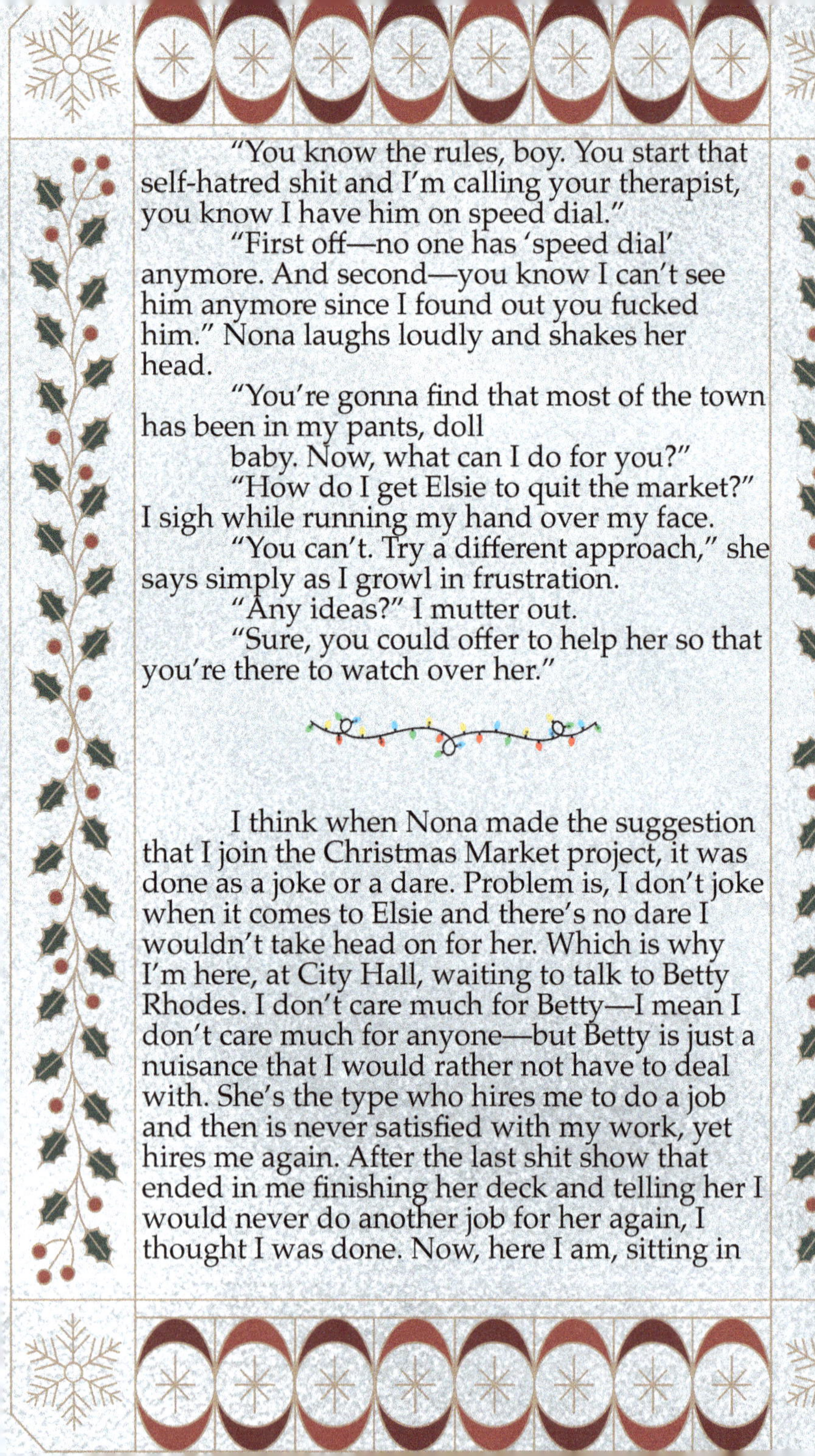

"You know the rules, boy. You start that self-hatred shit and I'm calling your therapist, you know I have him on speed dial."

"First off—no one has 'speed dial' anymore. And second—you know I can't see him anymore since I found out you fucked him." Nona laughs loudly and shakes her head.

"You're gonna find that most of the town has been in my pants, doll baby. Now, what can I do for you?"

"How do I get Elsie to quit the market?" I sigh while running my hand over my face.

"You can't. Try a different approach," she says simply as I growl in frustration.

"Any ideas?" I mutter out.

"Sure, you could offer to help her so that you're there to watch over her."

I think when Nona made the suggestion that I join the Christmas Market project, it was done as a joke or a dare. Problem is, I don't joke when it comes to Elsie and there's no dare I wouldn't take head on for her. Which is why I'm here, at City Hall, waiting to talk to Betty Rhodes. I don't care much for Betty—I mean I don't care much for anyone—but Betty is just a nuisance that I would rather not have to deal with. She's the type who hires me to do a job and then is never satisfied with my work, yet hires me again. After the last shit show that ended in me finishing her deck and telling her I would never do another job for her again, I thought I was done. Now, here I am, sitting in the chair in front of her desk as she wheels herself in.

"Grant, to what do I owe the pleasure?" she inquires, her drawn-on brow arched.

"Elsie Marshall," I say, not wanting to beat around the bush. "She's been chosen for the Christmas Marketplace."

"Yes," she states slowly. "With my current injury, I'm unable to give it the attention it needs and Elsie has been wanting to head the event for years, I think she'll be a great fit." That's a lie. Betty and Elsie couldn't be more opposite. Betty wants Elsie because she thinks she can manipulate her into following her orders.

"Fire her." Betty laughs in shock while shaking her head.

"What? Why? I have no one else to run this! I need the help, you of all people should understand my predicament." My jaw tenses at the jab about my leg. I let it roll off though. I've never asked for help—even when I should've. So her words—while sharp—won't pierce the protective armor I have in place.

"Then give me your spot," I state, already regretting my suggestion. "If you're so bad, make me the co-planner." At least this way I'll be able to keep an eye on Elsie, and I'll have a say in the decisions.

Betty scoffs while shaking her head. "And why on earth would I do that?"

"Because if you do—" *God I can't believe I'm about to offer this.* "If you do, I'll build your gazebo." Her entire body lights up and I know I have just made a deal with the Devil herself. But if it keeps Elsie safe, it's worth it.

Betty eyes me carefully, considering the offer. "Fine," she says at last, her voice

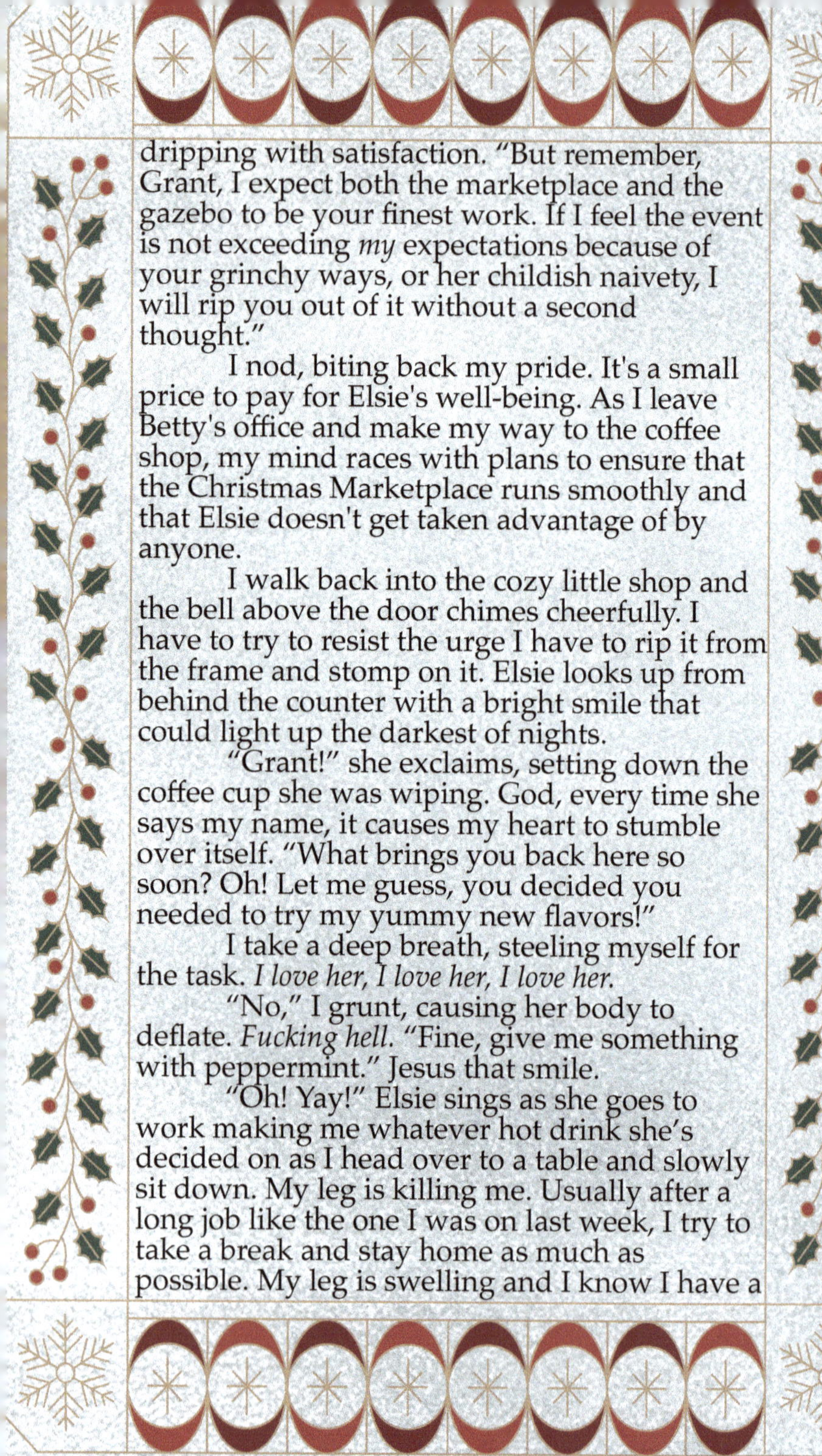

dripping with satisfaction. "But remember, Grant, I expect both the marketplace and the gazebo to be your finest work. If I feel the event is not exceeding *my* expectations because of your grinchy ways, or her childish naivety, I will rip you out of it without a second thought."

I nod, biting back my pride. It's a small price to pay for Elsie's well-being. As I leave Betty's office and make my way to the coffee shop, my mind races with plans to ensure that the Christmas Marketplace runs smoothly and that Elsie doesn't get taken advantage of by anyone.

I walk back into the cozy little shop and the bell above the door chimes cheerfully. I have to try to resist the urge I have to rip it from the frame and stomp on it. Elsie looks up from behind the counter with a bright smile that could light up the darkest of nights.

"Grant!" she exclaims, setting down the coffee cup she was wiping. God, every time she says my name, it causes my heart to stumble over itself. "What brings you back here so soon? Oh! Let me guess, you decided you needed to try my yummy new flavors!"

I take a deep breath, steeling myself for the task. *I love her, I love her, I love her.*

"No," I grunt, causing her body to deflate. *Fucking hell.* "Fine, give me something with peppermint." Jesus that smile.

"Oh! Yay!" Elsie sings as she goes to work making me whatever hot drink she's decided on as I head over to a table and slowly sit down. My leg is killing me. Usually after a long job like the one I was on last week, I try to take a break and stay home as much as possible. My leg is swelling and I know I have a sore forming which is making the prosthetic uncomfortable.

"You okay?" Elsie asks while sitting a cup in front of me along with a cookie I didn't ask for.

"Never better," I mutter, taking a sip of the drink which has too much whipped cream. Elsie giggles and I raise a brow. "What?"

She shakes her head and—*what in the fuck is she doing?* My breath hitches as her thumb runs over the corner of my mouth.

"You had a little whipped cream there." She laughs before sitting across from me. She casually pops her thumb into her mouth, sucking the whipped cream off of it. *Fuuuck this is an image that my cock will never let me forget.*

"You going to tell me why you're here?" she asks, still smiling and I notice a pink hue tinting her freckled cheeks. Fuck, she's so pretty.

"Needed another coffee," I state thickly while trying to discreetly adjust the semi I have happening in my jeans. She wrinkles her nose and shakes her head.

"Nice try. You've never changed your pattern, not even once. Always one at open and one at close. In fact, I remember bringing you coffee on job sites and telling you to let me know if you needed an afternoon pick-me-up and you stated that you needed more than three hours between my sugar in a cup."

"Fair," I mutter, taking another sip before leaning back in the chair to try and stretch out my leg. I should've driven, but I left my truck at City Hall so now I'm going to have to walk back there to get it.

"Is your leg hurting?" Her question is so caring and innocent but it fills me with ice cold anxiety.

"Betty is making me your partner on the Christmas marketplace," I blurt out, causing her to jolt back.

"Wait." Her red brows wrinkle together in confusion. "*My* project?"

"Yeah," I grunt, sipping the coffee again. It's actually pretty good. Then again, it's probably a pound of sugar so that's not shocking. "*Our* project now. I was talking to her today about a job and she said she couldn't help you or something and offered me the job."

"And what." She lets out a small chuckle. "You said yes? You—Grumpy Grant—are going to team up with me for the Christmas marketplace."

"Can you stop calling me that?" I groan and she shrugs while—*is she taking a drink of my coffee? Oh my god she is. Why is this almost as hot as her licking her thumb?* I stare in shock as she sets the mug back down.

"Stop being a grump and I will."

"I'm not a grump!" I huff. "I'm old, I'm tired and people are loud and annoying."

"You aren't that old—"

"Mileage, not the years, Els." I see a small, fond smile form on her pretty face. "What?"

"You are the only person who still calls me that. Everyone else calls me Ellie or Elsie."

The only person.

Because her brother was the other, and after he died, she screamed at anyone who called her that. Except me. I somehow got grandfathered in, and as much as that should make me happy, it doesn't. It doesn't, because

I'm the reason she switched from Els to Ellie. And I fucking hate Ellie. I mean, it's a pretty name, I guess. But it's not her name. It's not *my* name for her.

"I should go," I state—feeling overwhelmed. I stand and grunt in pain as my leg screams.

"Oh no!" Elsie's hands press my chest and shoulder. "Are you alright? Where's your truck?" She's got to stop touching me and I *really* need her and that warm scent of hers to stop suffocating me.

"I'm fine," I brush her off, wincing again. "I just need to get back over to City Hall."

"I'll take you!" she volunteers and moves to get her purse and coat.

"What? Elsie, no. I'll be—"

"I know you're a big, strong, independent man who's fully capable of doing big, strong, independent man things. But I'm either driving you to your truck, or following behind you while telling you just how silly it is that because you have a penis, you won't accept help from a woman." I blink, once, twice—I don't know, twenty-seven fucking times while trying to come up with my response.

"Never," I huff out as the heat floods my cheeks. "And I mean *never*, say penis to me again." Her giggle does nothing to aid in this uncomfortable feeling. "And second, it has nothing to do with you being a woman and everything to do with…" I trail off as I scratch the back of my neck.

"Truck giving you hell again?" she asks softly and I respond with a grunt. My old truck means everything to me, but the girl is not

doing well and I fear she's not going to make it through the winter. I got her to City Hall but it was a struggle, and I know if I try to start it up, she's not going to turn over and I don't have it in me to work on it while Elsie stands there watching.

"Come on, Grant." Her hand touches mine and I jerk it back in surprise.

"Sorry," I breathe out, embarrassment consuming me. "You startled me, sorry," I mutter again.

"Grant." She lets out a sigh before flipping the open sign and motioning to the door. "Come on, I'm taking you home." I want to fight her but Elsie isn't one to back down when her mind is set on something. So, I relent and follow her out of the coffee shop.

"I'm sorry you're having to do this," I say under my breath as she locks the door before stuffing her hands in her coat pockets.

"No need to be sorry! I offered!"

"Yeah, but, this is an inconvenience." I am an inconvenience.

"If it were an inconvenience, why would I have offered?" she asks while we round the corner to where she has her car parked. I notice that she's staying back at my slowed pace and it angers me. Not because it's not sweet—it is. And anyone else who hasn't spent the years I have, watching her every move like some kind of psychotic stalker wouldn't notice. But I have, and I notice. Elsie is a fast walker, especially when it's cold outside. As much as she loves this time of year, she hates the cold and her little body doesn't retain much heat. But she knows I'm in too much pain, she knows I can't move faster, so she's slowed her pace to match mine, and it makes me want to yell at her.

"Ah!" Elsie cries as she hits a patch of ice and her feet go out from under her. Without thinking, I grab her upper arm to stop her from hitting the concrete sidewalk, but in doing so, I lose my footing and fall into a shoveled snow pile with Elsie landing roughly on top of me, her knee hitting my nuts so perfectly I think I might've died momentarily.

She does a small wiggle as she moves to sit up. "Fuck," I gasp in a far less than manly way, but I mean, my testicles are in my fucking throat right now, I should be allowed this moment.

"Oh my god," she gasps. "Did I break your ribs?" Instantly she tries to move again. And *again* puts more force on my nuts. I reach out and grip her thigh while trying to remember how to breathe.

"For the love of…" I'm going to throw up, I swear to fucking Christ. "I'm in pain because every time you move, your knee digs deeper into my nuts. Please… stop… moving." She looks down between us before whipping her head back up and I can almost hear her telepathically begging me to feel her apology. Evidently I either don't look like I hear it, or I don't look like I forgive her because she begins verbally begging.

"I am so so so—"

"Els," I state dryly while resting my head in the snow. "Stop talking."

"I know but, I'm nervous and you know the more nervous I get the more I—"

"Stop moving that mouth or I'll do it for you." My voice is low and firm as I tighten my grip on her thigh. Her eyes go wide and her cheeks go red as she closes her pretty lips. Well, for half a second.

"How do I get off?" she whispers and I feel her shaking slightly due to being as still as possible.

"Right," I breathe out. "The leg I'm holding." *The silky soft leg that I want to wear around my face like a goddamn scarf—No! Grant, fucking shut up. You're not doing this! She may have broken your dick and re-homed your testicles. You are not thinking this shit right now!* "Move it straight back," I say over the two lumps wedged firmly in my throat. She obeys—too quickly, and I let out a whimper as she gets off.

"Oh my god, Grant." She holds her hand out and, what is she going to do? She can't lift me, she can't— "Take my fucking hand, you butthead!" She snaps and… that's not hot, that's *not* hot. I grab her icy hand as she impressively pulls me up.

"You're strong for such a little thing," I rasp out, unable to straighten fully.

"I work out… sometimes," she huffs before opening the door to a green Prius.

"You're joking," I state flatly while limping over to the toy car. "W-Where is your car?"

"In the shop. It needed something done to it. I don't know, I tried to change the fluid and then it stopped working."

Scrunching myself into this matchbox on wheels, I feel almost claustrophobic as I close the door. "What fluid?" I ask as she gets in and starts the engine.

"Uhhh…" She laughs uncomfortably while scratching her head. "Well, I was going to start with the oil and I was trying to follow the guy online and I don't know, I twisted some stuff under the car and liquid started rushing out and—Oh I don't know! You know I suck with car stuff. That was yours and David's thing. I can't figure it out." She laughs but I don't reciprocate. Mainly because she mentioned *his* name again. She says it so easily, like a knife isn't being stabbed into her heart every time. Then again, maybe it isn't. Maybe I'm the only one who feels this way because I'm the guilty party.

3

GRANT

"I appreciate you doing this," I force out as Elsie parks her car in front of my house. "Let me give you some money for gas."

"Grant." She chuckles, shaking her head. "It took fifteen minutes and it's a hybrid. I don't need gas money. Now, let me help you inside." Panic fills me at her words. Her? Alone? In my house? Yeah, no… abso-fucking-lutely not happening.

"I would rather just go inside and ice my leg and nuts, Els, but than—" The driver's door shuts as Elsie—completely ignoring me—starts strolling up to my steps. I notice a

slight limp and wonder if she hurt herself in the fall.

Contorting myself out of the tiny-ass car, I make my way toward her. "Are you alright?" I ask while climbing the couple steps that lead onto the front porch of my snow-covered bungalow.

"Yeah, why?" She beams up at me as I unlock the door.

"You're limping," I point out, gesturing to her leg as we walk in and she instantly removes her snow covered shoes, leaving them on the mat by the door.

"Oh it's nothing—" Her voice trails off as she looks around expectantly. "What on earth is going on here?"

"What?" I ask, feeling almost defensive. What's wrong with my house? It's a nice house, I keep it up-to-date and it's relatively clean.

"Where are the Christmas decorations? Where's your tree?" *Oh for fucksake.*

"Un-purchased and at the store where they belong," I mutter while moving past her to my couch. I sit at the end with the chaise as I begin unzipping the interior zipper of my pant leg. "You don't have to be here for this," I mutter, feeling exposed. It's not a secret about my prosthetic—obviously. She's seen it. Fuck she's seen the worst of the worst. But still, removing the prosthesis, the socket and liner—it's not necessarily the sexiest position I've been in.

"Here for what?" she asks, partially distracted as she wanders around my living room. "This would be perfect for those old-school Christmas lights." She beams, while running her fingers over my mantle. "Honestly, I feel like your house would be amazing with the old, colorful lights, lots of red and green…" She trails off as she turns toward me while I slide the sleeve off my leg and let out a hiss in pain.

"Yeah, ain't happening." I chuckle to mask my discomfort as I rest back against the couch pillow. I look at her, expecting to see her staring at my leg, but she's not. She's taking her coat off and hanging it up by the door before lightly limping back to me.

"I'll get you some ice."

"I'm fine," I say softly. "I'll take some painkillers and elevate it." She wrinkles her nose while giggling lightly.

"I meant for your nuts." I feel the heat rush to my cheeks at her statement. She walks to the kitchen and returns after a moment with a plastic bag of ice and a kitchen towel.

"Thanks," I say while placing the bag on my crotch. She sits on the couch next to me and I think I make it to the count of twelve before she inhales to begin her nervous chatter. She's been doing this since we were kids and her dad was still around. Silence always meant she was going to be in trouble by him, so she continuously talked in hopes it would distract him. It rarely ever did.

"You know what you need?" she starts, and I roll my eyes.

"I don't want Christmas decorations," I groan as she huffs.

"First off, those *are* happening. We can't have Project Chestnuts happening in an unseasonal location. No, headquarters has to be top notch for photo ops." A–Am I having a stroke?

"Headquarters? Project Chestnuts? Els, what are you talking about?"

"Project Chestnuts is the name of the Christmas Marketplace project. Like it? I just came up with it."

"Why chestnuts? Why not just call it the 'Christmas Marketplace Project'?" *Why am I humoring this? I don't care why? Why is she still here is the question I need to be asking.*

"Chest." Elsie pokes her beautiful— emphasis on the full—breasts. "And nuts!" She points to my sore crotch.

"I don't want to play anymore," I groan as she giggles excitedly. "Fine," I relent, but only because that sweet little laugh is my fucking kryptonite. "Why is my house the headquarters? And what in the fuck makes you think there will be any photos taken in here?"

"There *will* be pictures, because memories are important and some day you may want to look back on them." Her voice holds a tone that hits me in the gut. She shakes her head before shrugging. "And it's

either your place or mine and seeing as I
am kind of without a place to live at the
moment…" She trails off and I watch her
tuck her coppery hair behind her ears—it's
a tic of hers, she has a couple that I've
watched develop since we were kids. Hair
behind the ears, popping her knuckles
individually three complete times, and if
she's really bad, she starts counting things
while tapping her fingers against her
thumb.

"Why not stay with Nona?" I ask,
trying to get her moving past the sad
thoughts.

"Ha! Are you insane!" She laughs
while curling her legs up onto the couch
cushion. My chest is doing this weird
tightening thing that I'm sure warrants a
call to my doctor. "I ain't staying with that
crazy woman and whatever gentleman or
lady callers she brings home for the night!"
I shudder at the thought. Nona is a—
worldly woman. She's been fighting and
protesting for women's rights all over the
country for decades, though her tactics are
a bit unorthodox. While some believe in
signs and human barriers, Nona was out
there setting things on fire and holding
public orgies. While she doesn't protest
anymore her… ummm… *desires* haven't
diminished with age and she's often seen
with other men, women, or groups.
Honestly it's not what you'd expect in this
quiet, Hallmark looking town, but I'm
pretty sure Nona either secretly owns the

town or has dirt on the people who do because no one bats an eye at the eighty-something, heavily tattooed, no bra wearing woman.

"Valid," I state, rubbing my aching thigh.

"You never let me finish my statement," she says while rubbing her eye. I wonder if the contacts she's wearing are bothering her. Elsie has terrible vision and usually has on glasses. She looks so fucking adorable in them. But over the last month I've noticed her switching to contacts, I also have noticed she's constantly rubbing and blinking her eyes to adjust them. "Do you know what you need?"

"Right now? A large pizza and a nap."

"Oh that sounds delicious, but no. You need a friend." I scoff at her suggestion as the hairs on the back of my neck prickle and stand on end.

"If this is you offering—"

"Shut up, I'm the best friend you got." She swats my bicep and I raise my brow.

"We aren't even friends."

"Woah, excuse the mess but my heart just shattered all over your floor," she states dryly and I give her a low chuckle before she continues. "No you need a fur-baby, like a dog."

"Hard pass." I reach into my pocket and pull out my phone to find something—anything to do besides have this conversation. I don't want friends—human or otherwise.

"Well, I think a friend would be good for you." She smiles while standing. "Along with some Christmas decorations." Sighing, I drop my phone down as I glare up at her.

"Well, maybe this is a time of the year I'd rather forget," I snap out and watch as the color and playfulness leave her face. "Maybe, I would rather not think about the last time I had lights up, or a tree. Maybe I would rather not think about the last time I had a fucking friend. Maybe Elsie, just maybe, I do the things I do to keep going and I don't need you coming along and fucking it up with your suggestions. Don't you fucking get it? I want to be left the fuck alone!" I hear the *pop pop pop* of her knuckles as her lip quivers while her eyes go glassy.

"Fuck, Els—" She waves me off and forces a smile which squeezes the tears from her eyes.

"I should go. I-If you need a ride to your tr—" She pauses while grabbing her coat. "Right, you'll find a way, without my help. Have a good night, Grant."

"Elsie, goddamnit, wait!" I call out as I reach for my crutch. It's too late, though, she's already in her car and driving back down to town, leaving me here with a pit in my stomach and chest pain that could be a heart attack. Why didn't I humor her? I finally had her in my house, she said pizza

sounded good. I could've ordered us some, this could've been an unofficial date and yet…

"You fucking moron."

4

ELSIE

SIX YEARS AGO

"Els, I don't care!" My brother David sighs in irritation as we continue down the road back into town. "You should've never gone to that party alone."

"I'm an adult," I hum in annoyance, though I know he's right, the moment I got there I was ready to go. Everyone was having sex with everyone and the drugs were everywhere. I called David the second I saw some guy I didn't know slip something in my drink. I left and started walking until David got to me. "But you're right, I should… David?" I pat his arm and point to the other side of the highway. "Is that Grant's motorcycle?" I adjust my glasses. It's hard to see in the dark but I swear that's his custom green paint job gleaming under the street light.

"Fuck, it is." David pulls over and whips open his truck door. "Stay put unless I yell for you." I nod as he runs through the median and to the further lane.

Leaning over the center console, I push my glasses up the bridge of my nose as I watch my brother try to move the fallen motorcycle off our friend. I hear Grant's painful scream from here and it churns my stomach. He must be badly injured. I hurry and pull out my cell phone, dialing 911. I listen to it ring while watching as David lets go and backs away.

"911, what's your emergency?" The male voice on the other end grabs my attention.

"Y-Yeah, there's been an accident, northbound on I-27, the man is trapped under his motorcycle. By mile marker 198." The guy says something, but lights in the distance distract me. I look from David— who is running backward while yelling something at Grant—to the lights… the lights of a semi.

"Oh no," I breathe, frantically trying to rip my seatbelt off.

"Ma'am?"

"No! DAVID!" I scream while blaring the horn. David turns to look at me as the semi hits. "No! OH GOD!" I shriek as I get out of the car and run through the median. I try to go to David but the trucker is holding me back, his body shaking.

"Darling, you can't see this, stay back." I don't know what keeps me from fighting him, but I stumble again and head over to Grant.

"What… happened?" he wheezes through his helmet. I look at his leg pinned under his bike and let out a whimper. It looks so bad, and I can't tell if the dark wet spots I see are his blood or fluid from the motorcycle.

"Grant." I glance up to see my brother's motionless feet on the road in front of the truck. "He… The truck hit him. H—He's…" His shaky, icy hand covers mine and gives me the weakest squeeze.

"Shhh… Listen, sweetheart, it's going to be okay." His words are slurred and faint as he tries to speak. I look at the blood he's losing and choke on a sob. Both of them are going to leave me. I'm going to be left alone. I can't do this, I can—

"Come here," he murmurs, pulling me to his chest like he used to when my dad would yell or hit me. The difference this time is his once strong heartbeat is now so shallow. "Atta girl." His hand goes into my hair as he holds me to him. "How many—" He wheezes as he tries to speak. "How many teeth are on my zipper?" I look at his pretty blue eyes as they begin to roll and I want to take his helmet off. I want to but I don't—he could have a spine injury and I shouldn't even be touching him right now, let alone moving his neck.

"Grant please," I beg through my sobs. "Please, please, please. I can't lose the only two men I've ever loved at the same time. Please. You can't leave me. I'll never fucking forgive you."

"Count, sweetheart." His hand grips my hair as I lay back on his chest, listening as the sirens sound off in the distance.

"One, two, three…"

Present

The ding of the bell pulls me from my thoughts as I look up and see Lance, a foreman who works for Grant. He's a nice guy, big and broad with a warm smile, dark skin and kind eyes. It's always a treat when he comes in—mainly because he likes my fun new pastries.

"Ellie." His voice booms through the shop. "When are you going to stop playing hard to get and marry me?" Oh, and he's a shameless flirt. I blush and giggle while staring up at him. "I'm pretty sure your hubby might have a problem with that."

Lance rolls his eyes as he leans on the counter. "Listen, I'll leave him in a heartbeat if I can get you to move in and start making me breakfast." I laugh lightly as the bell rings again. I turn to greet the customer, only to see it's Grant. I haven't seen him since I took him home two days ago when he shouted at me to leave him alone. It's not the first time he's said that to me. It's the second, actually. The first was in the hospital after he was in recovery. They had to amputate his leg above the knee, and with the trauma and blood loss, they didn't expect him to live. David was dead the second the truck hit him—thankfully. They said he didn't suffer, he probably hadn't even registered the hit. It's just Grant and I who had to live with the memory.

"Oh." Lance straightens up and smirks at Grant. "Hey, Boss, I could've grabbed you something." Grant waves him off.

"It's fine, I needed to talk to Elsie anyway." *Oh god, why?*

Lance must sense the awkwardness because he asks for a simple order and leaves with the shortest goodbye we've ever had.

"Good Morning, Grant," I state crisply while grabbing a cup. "Black coffee, no extras, no happiness—right?" I all but shove the plain white cup in his hands.

"Els, can we talk for a second?" I shake my head before turning around to restock my cups.

"Sorry, I'm busy and I have to get ready to head to the square to meet with some potential vendors."

"Well, I'm your partner—why didn't you tell me so I could go?" I let out a loud sigh before glaring at him, which is hard to do in these stupid contacts, but the last guy

I went out with said my glasses gave me a nerdy mom look. I don't really know what that means but I'm assuming since I never heard from him again, it must not be a good thing.

"Well gee, Grant, maybe it's because I finally fucking got it and I'm leaving you alone." I rip my apron off before storming to the back of the shop where I've turned the small break area into a bedroom.

"Elsie, would you just—" His voice trails off when he sees the room. "Are you… Els come on, you can't be living here like this."

"It's fine." I pop my knuckles as I feel the walls closing in on me.

"Elsie, listen—"

"No!" I shout, hitting his chest. "You're not the only one who lost someone that night, Grant! So fuck you for being so damn selfish!"

"I'm being selfish?" he says as though offended. "I know he was your brother, but he was all I had too, Elsie, and it's not fair that you think the way I deal with that loss is wrong. I don't go to you and tell you that you need to take off your mask."

"I'm not wearing a mask!"

"Ohh, you're wearing a mask," he huffs out. "Little Miss *Ellie* with rainbows and sunshine. *Please*. It's completely fake."

"I am happy!" I shout, shoving him out of the way so I can storm around him and walk back to the main area.

"Oh yeah, you're the epitome of happiness!"

"Rather that than be the human version of the grumpy cat meme."

"I don't know what that even means," he hisses back and I roll my eyes before crying in frustration as my contact falls out.

"Damn it!"

"What's wrong?" he asks as I close my eye so I can see him clearer.

"My contact fell out," I groan loudly. "It was my last pair."

"Why do you wear them if they're so uncomfortable?" he asks as I walk to the employee bathroom to remove the other contact. Once it's out, I put my thick rimmed glasses on and come back out.

"It doesn't matter, anyway, I gotta go."

"Els—"

"What, Grant?" I snap, feeling overwhelmed. Why can't he just leave *me* alone? He wanted me to fuck off—I fucked off! Why is he here now talking to me in that sweet way like he did during the accident? I don't want it!

"I'm sorry I hurt your feelings the other day." He shifts uncomfortably while rubbing the back of his neck. "Really, I just…"

"Save it," I breathe out while releasing the frustration. "I get it, I came into your house and became overwhelming, I deserved it. But please,

can we just drop this because I really do have a meeting at the square to meet a potential vendor." His brows furrow while he looks at me as if he doesn't believe me but he straightens and gives me a nod.

"Alright, I'll drive you." I open my mouth to argue but I know there's no point, so I smile and nod while following him out to his truck. I walk to the passenger side and pause as my hand reaches for the handle on the door. Taking a breath, I open the door and see the black marker on the floorboard where I had drawn a flower to piss David off, when this was his truck.

"You alright?" Grant asks from the driver's seat. I can't get in there. I can't get in this truck, and yet Grant can't walk to the square, his leg is probably still hurting from the other day and there's a thick blanket of snow on the ground.

"I'll meet you there," I manage to get out as I back away from the truck and start walking. I hear Grant cussing and yelling at me to turn around but I ignore him as I continue to walk through the snow-covered town while trying to calm my thoughts.

"*DAVID!*"

I flinch at the voice in my head—*my voice*—screaming for my big brother in that truck.

"Don't do this Elsie," I whisper to myself. "You're stronger than your grief. You've got this." Looking down at my boots disappearing in the snow, I begin to count

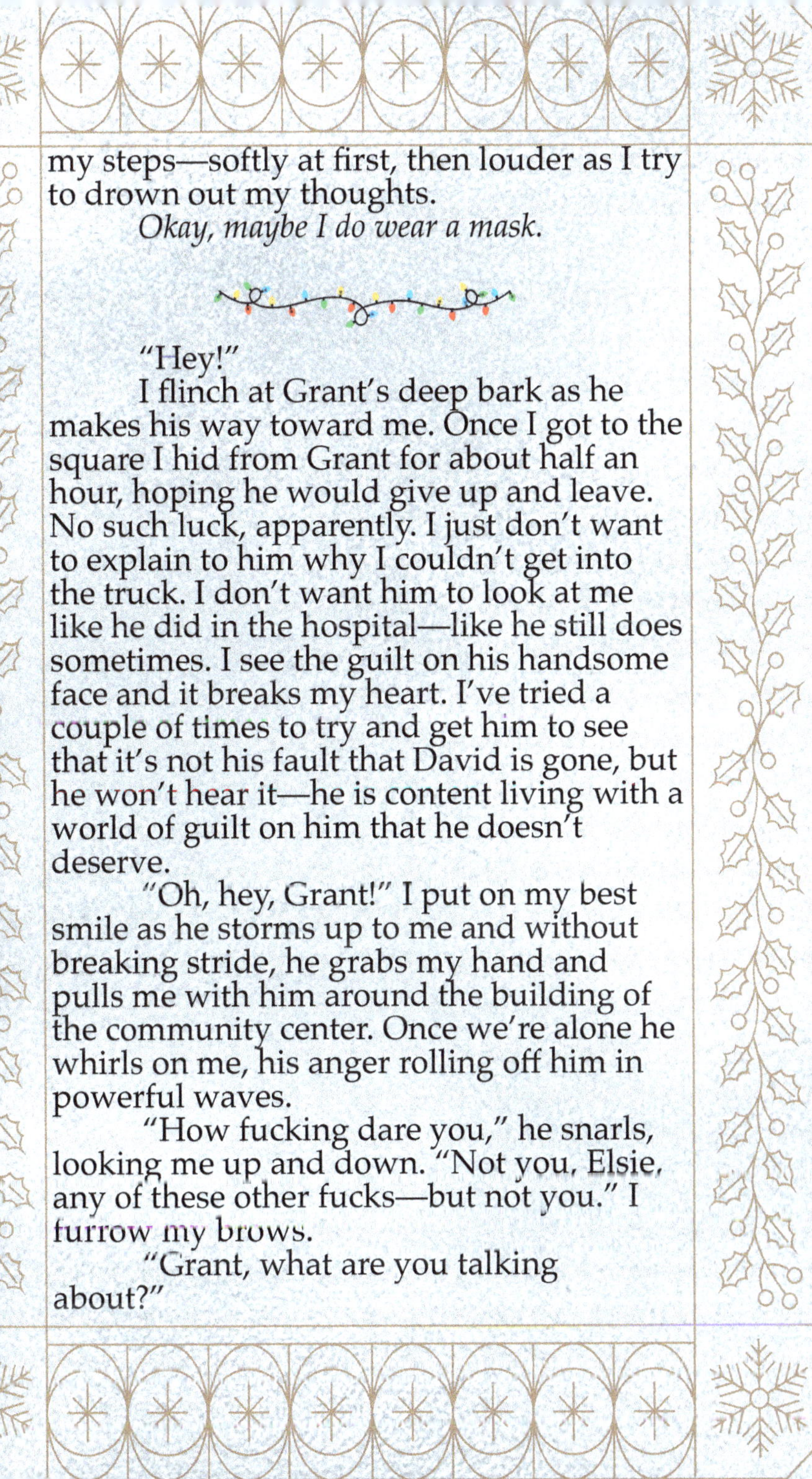

my steps—softly at first, then louder as I try to drown out my thoughts.

Okay, maybe I do wear a mask.

"Hey!"

I flinch at Grant's deep bark as he makes his way toward me. Once I got to the square I hid from Grant for about half an hour, hoping he would give up and leave. No such luck, apparently. I just don't want to explain to him why I couldn't get into the truck. I don't want him to look at me like he did in the hospital—like he still does sometimes. I see the guilt on his handsome face and it breaks my heart. I've tried a couple of times to try and get him to see that it's not his fault that David is gone, but he won't hear it—he is content living with a world of guilt on him that he doesn't deserve.

"Oh, hey, Grant!" I put on my best smile as he storms up to me and without breaking stride, he grabs my hand and pulls me with him around the building of the community center. Once we're alone he whirls on me, his anger rolling off him in powerful waves.

"How fucking dare you," he snarls, looking me up and down. "Not you, Elsie, any of these other fucks—but not you." I furrow my brows.

"Grant, what are you talking about?"

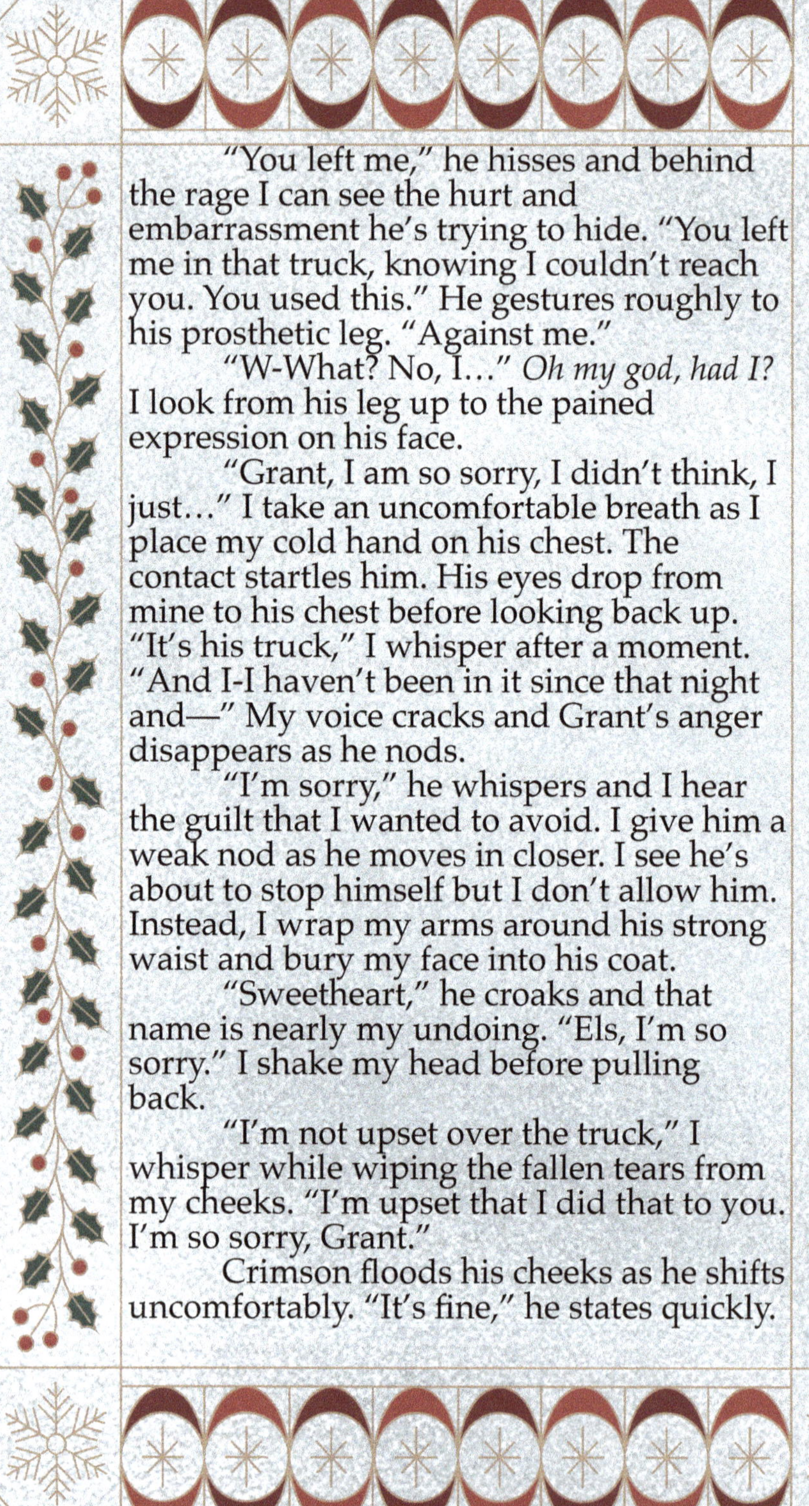

"You left me," he hisses and behind the rage I can see the hurt and embarrassment he's trying to hide. "You left me in that truck, knowing I couldn't reach you. You used this." He gestures roughly to his prosthetic leg. "Against me."

"W-What? No, I…" *Oh my god, had I?* I look from his leg up to the pained expression on his face.

"Grant, I am so sorry, I didn't think, I just…" I take an uncomfortable breath as I place my cold hand on his chest. The contact startles him. His eyes drop from mine to his chest before looking back up. "It's his truck," I whisper after a moment. "And I-I haven't been in it since that night and—" My voice cracks and Grant's anger disappears as he nods.

"I'm sorry," he whispers and I hear the guilt that I wanted to avoid. I give him a weak nod as he moves in closer. I see he's about to stop himself but I don't allow him. Instead, I wrap my arms around his strong waist and bury my face into his coat.

"Sweetheart," he croaks and that name is nearly my undoing. "Els, I'm so sorry." I shake my head before pulling back.

"I'm not upset over the truck," I whisper while wiping the fallen tears from my cheeks. "I'm upset that I did that to you. I'm so sorry, Grant."

Crimson floods his cheeks as he shifts uncomfortably. "It's fine," he states quickly.

"No, it's not! I hurt your feelings!" This seems to embarrass him further. I remove my hand and give him an apologetic smile. "How about we just meet the vendors. I'm sure they're going to be less than thrilled that I've kept them waiting."

He studies me for a moment before nodding. "You know, they're only here to suck the happiness and joy out of you, right?"

I gently elbow him in his side. "Well, luckily my happiness is a mask, right?"

PAGE BREAK

I'm going to have to quit.

As I sit here, listening for the thirtieth time about why a vendor should be getting a coveted front booth at the market, all I can think is—I'm not made to tell people no. Today is just a small meeting of a few repeat vendors. I have to do this again, multiple times, and if I gave everyone a front spot who has asked today alone, I would've been telling people no thirty minutes ago.

"Els?" Grant's voice is a soft whisper that pulls me back into reality. I look at him as he sits next to me at the table. I must have a *save me* expression on my face because his features harden before turning back to Michelle Lyons of *Lyon's Quilts* and giving her a curt nod. "We'll be in touch," he states and Michelle huffs indignantly while shaking her head. I notice her short bob doesn't sway the slightest as she does

so. *I wonder how much hairspray she uses to turn her hair into a literal helmet.*

"Excuse me?" Her eyes narrow. "Lyon's Quilts has been a first booth staple for fifteen years! You can't possibl—"

"I'm not possibly doing anything," Grant states calmly and I jump as I feel his hand grip mine under the table. He runs his thumb over my knuckles and—ow, they're tender. *How long have I been trying to crack my knuckles?* "I'm telling you we'll be in touch. We haven't met with all the clients yet and haven't made decisions on vendor placement." Michelle glares at Grant and I'm about to apologize when his grip tightens on my hand. "Have a great day," his voice is firm and final as they both share a hard stare before Michelle finally blinks and storms away.

"Let's go outside," he whispers in my ear and I nod, following him out of the community center. Once the cool air hits my heated face, I feel like I am finally able to breathe.

"That was so intense," I whisper, running my hands through my hair and tucking strands behind my ears.

"Are you alright?" *His voice…* ugh, when Grant uses that deep, soothing tone, I swear I'm melted chocolate.

"Yeah," I squeak out as he grips my hand in his again. I look down to see him taking his gloves from his coat pocket and slipping my hands in them. "Oh! Grant you don't have to—"

"Hush," he mutters, going to the other hand. "I wouldn't have to if you owned a pair of gloves," I scoff and roll my eyes.

"You know I don't believe in gloves." He eyes me and I feel my cheeks redden further.

"Yes, I'm aware of your lunacy."

"Grant," I huff in indignation. "Gloves are a conspiracy. You buy them, wear them once and then lose one. Then you have to go and buy more gloves just so the cycle can continue. Same with socks."

"Mhm…" he mutters while we walk down the square in a somewhat comfortable silence. As comfortable as a silence that includes me can be. I don't handle silence very well. I never have. When I was a kid, I used to turn on my music and blast my headphones as loud as possible to drown out my dad fighting with David or Nona. Or to escape the thoughts that would creep in after he would hurt me. I still do, but now it's not because of my abusive dad, it's because I don't have David, and I'm stuck with that final memory that lives on repeat in my head.

"Shit," Grant mutters at the same time I see the handwritten sign.

Northbrook Animal Shelter
Christmas Adoption

"Oh my God," I breathe, my body vibrating. "They have puppers! I'm petting them all!" I see the apprehension on his face and give him a small smile. "You don't have to go with me. But I'm going over there and hugging all of the dogs."

5

GRANT

Sitting on the ice-cold, metal folding chair, I continue to attempt my scowl as Elsie makes good on her promise to hug every single dog at this event.

Every. Single. One.

The second I saw the sign for the adoption event, I knew three things were about to happen: First, Elsie was going to spend the rest of the day here. Second, I was going to have to figure out a way to get these people in the Christmas market or Elsie would lose her fucking shit and Third, she's going to trying to get me to adopt a dog.

She has tried, multiple times. She's walked by with at least ten different puppies

and I don't know, they're cute and all, but not my thing. I like dogs, I would love to have one, but I'm not someone who can always give them the exercise they need. I'm not gentle on my body in my line of work. I'm constantly moving the wrong way, putting too much weight on my prosthetic and just trying to be an average thirty-one year old man. But by doing that, I end up with sores, blisters, severe pain and swelling. Having a puppy I would have to run after—it's too much.

I watch as Elsie talks excitedly with the shelter coordinator. She's in her element here. Working with animals, working for a good cause—this is the Els I love. She was so anxious dealing with the vendors, which I knew she would be. And part of that was probably my fault. I didn't think about the truck, and I was so mad at her for walking away. I felt so helpless and it pissed me off. I don't want her to see me as weak, I want her to feel safe with me and highlighting the fact that running after her in the snow she was trekking through with this prosthesis—I would've ended up fucking my leg up. But when she mentioned the truck—it broke my heart.

The truck belongs to the company David and I started about six months before he passed. It's the company I still run today. After everything that happened—his death, the staggering bills I endured, and all the therapy I went through to learn to walk and use my prosthetic, I couldn't afford another vehicle. I mean hell, I was giving Nona and Elsie everything I could and forgoing food if need be. It's only been the last two years that I've paid everything off and am turning a decent profit so, the company truck was all I had and now—I guess I just didn't think about what it represented to her. Now I want to go set it on fire so she never has to look at it again.

I hear a grunt and a sigh next to me and look to see the blueish-grey and white face of a grown pitbull resting its head on my prosthetic leg. I glance around, expecting to see Els standing next to it, showing it off like the others—but I don't. Els is still talking to the shelter coordinator while holding some tiny ball of fur. The dog whimpers softly while scooting closer.

"Hey buddy." I extend my hand and it shivers in excitement as I pat its head.

"Oh! Holly!" I look up to see the coordinator and Elsie walking over. "I'm sorry! She's not supposed to be out of her pin," the older woman says softly and I feel the dog tuck closer to me.

"It's alright, she isn't bothering me," I say, petting her head again. The woman gives me a soft smile.

"She tends to make people nervous due to her size, so we keep her pinned. She's really sweet but has a bit of a timid side. She was a fighting dog that we rescued about two years ago so she doesn't like other animals. She also gets nervous

with loud voices so she's been returned several times."

"Awww, that's so sad," Elsie says looking at the dog. "How old is she?"

"About four, and because we have to disclose everything with her history, she doesn't get looked at much. We mainly take her to the events to give her some time out."

"Time out?" I huff looking at the woman. "Like a prisoner getting a treat? And what a treat it is to be overlooked for the puppies because you have scars." I look at the brown-eyed dog, her ears shivering as she looks at me. "You bring her out here, get her hopes up just to toss her back in the kennel?"

"Grant!" Elsie hisses but I wave my hand to stop her.

"She's coming with me," I state firmly before I can stop myself. Both the women stare blankly at me.

"W-What?" The coordinator looks from me to Elsie. "Is he serious? I thought you said he didn't want a dog?"

"I didn't," I confirm. "But she wants me and I'm not allowing her to go back to the shelter. Give me the paperwork, I'll fill out whatever and then I'm taking her home."

"Not one fucking word," I warn as Elsie gets out of her car with Holly. After I filled out the paperwork, I was given a sheet of things to get her, like food, treats and toys. So after Els promised she wouldn't leave Holly alone, I drove to the pet shop and I might've went overboard, but fuck I don't know, I feel like the girl deserves some nice shit after what she's been through. So my house is now equipped with all the toys, beds, and treats a dog could want. And if there's something I'm missing, I'll get it. Holly isn't going to ever fear going back to that shelter again.

Elsie's cheshire cat grin widens as she walks with Holly on a leash to my front porch. Holly is timid and scared until she sees me. She lets out a whimper and Elsie lets her leash go as the dog runs to me, sitting at my feet.

"Hey girl," I chuckle, petting her head. "Come on, let's see if this place is to your liking. *And you*—" I point my finger to the chuckling girl. "Not a word," As we walk in, I hear a small gasp escape Elsie. Holly doesn't leave my side as we enter the living room and I frown.

"I thought she'd be more excited about the toys," I mutter while watching her. Holly looks up at me as she tucks herself closer to my leg, her body shivering lightly.

"She's not used to being here, or having toys, there will be an adjustment period." Elsie pats my shoulder as I walk

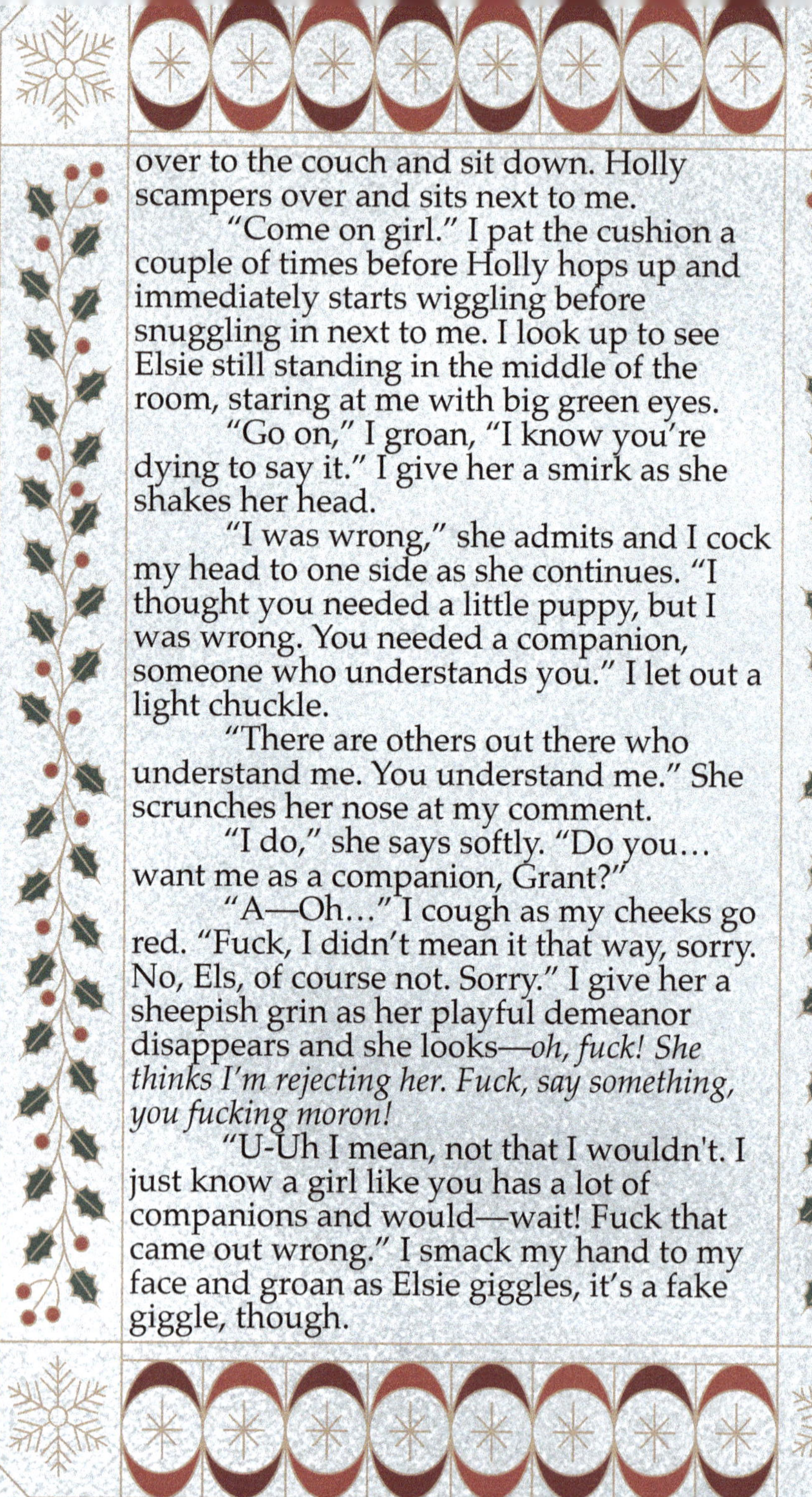

over to the couch and sit down. Holly scampers over and sits next to me.

"Come on girl." I pat the cushion a couple of times before Holly hops up and immediately starts wiggling before snuggling in next to me. I look up to see Elsie still standing in the middle of the room, staring at me with big green eyes.

"Go on," I groan, "I know you're dying to say it." I give her a smirk as she shakes her head.

"I was wrong," she admits and I cock my head to one side as she continues. "I thought you needed a little puppy, but I was wrong. You needed a companion, someone who understands you." I let out a light chuckle.

"There are others out there who understand me. You understand me." She scrunches her nose at my comment.

"I do," she says softly. "Do you… want me as a companion, Grant?"

"A—Oh…" I cough as my cheeks go red. "Fuck, I didn't mean it that way, sorry. No, Els, of course not. Sorry." I give her a sheepish grin as her playful demeanor disappears and she looks—*oh, fuck! She thinks I'm rejecting her. Fuck, say something, you fucking moron!*

"U-Uh I mean, not that I wouldn't. I just know a girl like you has a lot of companions and would—wait! Fuck that came out wrong." I smack my hand to my face and groan as Elsie giggles, it's a fake giggle, though.

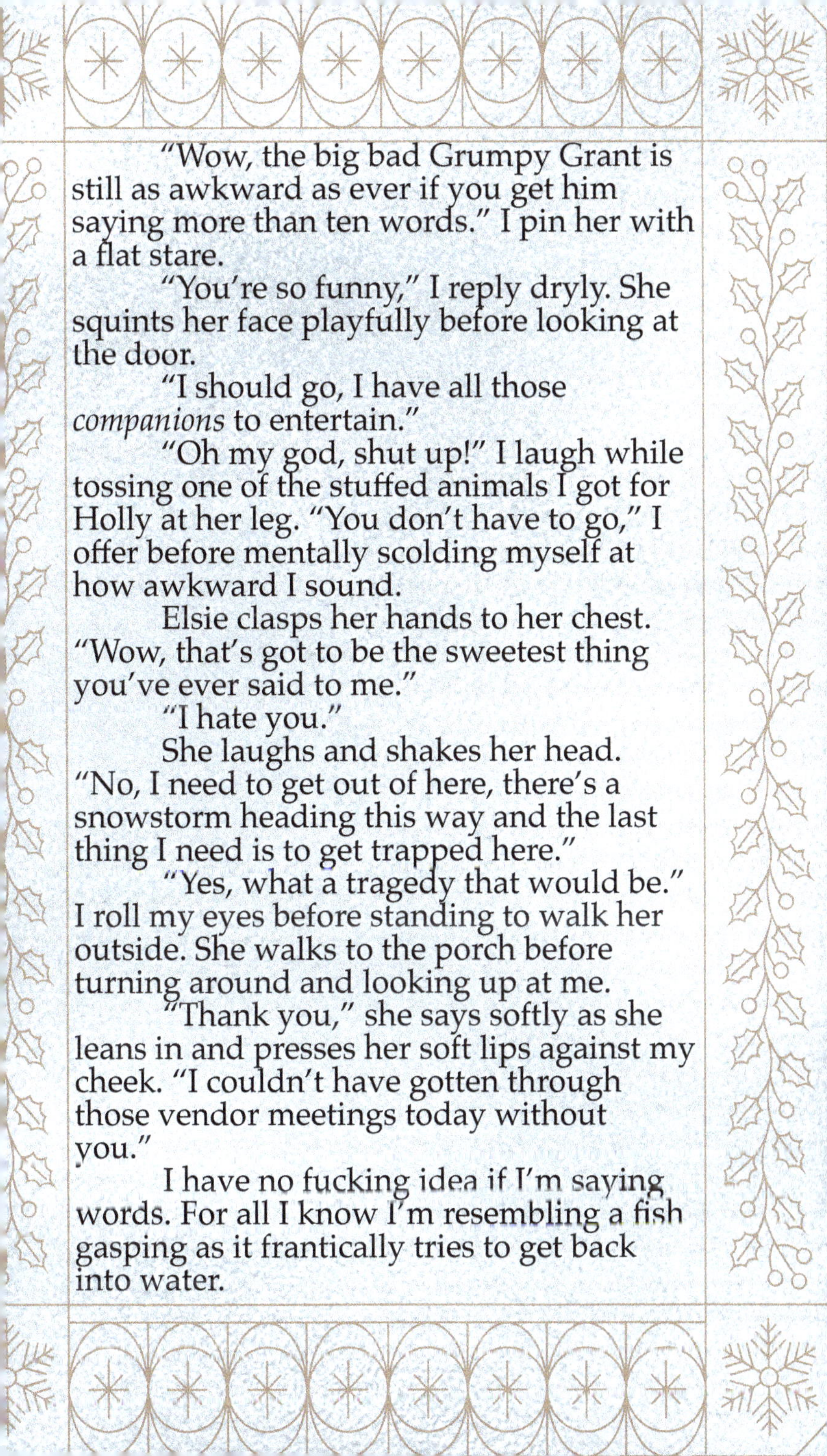

"Wow, the big bad Grumpy Grant is still as awkward as ever if you get him saying more than ten words." I pin her with a flat stare.

"You're so funny," I reply dryly. She squints her face playfully before looking at the door.

"I should go, I have all those *companions* to entertain."

"Oh my god, shut up!" I laugh while tossing one of the stuffed animals I got for Holly at her leg. "You don't have to go," I offer before mentally scolding myself at how awkward I sound.

Elsie clasps her hands to her chest. "Wow, that's got to be the sweetest thing you've ever said to me."

"I hate you."

She laughs and shakes her head. "No, I need to get out of here, there's a snowstorm heading this way and the last thing I need is to get trapped here."

"Yes, what a tragedy that would be." I roll my eyes before standing to walk her outside. She walks to the porch before turning around and looking up at me.

"Thank you," she says softly as she leans in and presses her soft lips against my cheek. "I couldn't have gotten through those vendor meetings today without you."

I have no fucking idea if I'm saying words. For all I know I'm resembling a fish gasping as it frantically tries to get back into water.

"Elsie," I manage to get out. She turns around to look at me and I see it on her pretty face. She wants me to tell her to stay. I know it. I may be an awkward mess around her but I know that look. If I ask her to, she'll come back inside. *Do it, you fucking moron, this is your chance.* "Text me when you get to your shop." I hate how much of a coward I am. She deflates as I knew she would but gives me a nod before getting into that stupid ass loaner and backing out of the driveway. I release a painful sigh as I turn around and head back inside. Holly is in the same spot and I notice the nervous look on her face.

"Hey girl." I smile as I walk over to her. "You want something to eat?" I see her look out my window that looks outside where Elsie's car was.

"Yeah, you'll find I'm not the smoothest when it comes to her."

"Hello?" I groan as I answer my ringing phone. After Elsie left, I fed Holly and then I guess she and I fell asleep on the couch. The living room is dark so I must've been out for a couple hours.

"Grant." The panic in Nona's voice is the bucket of ice water I need to wake up. "Please tell me Elsie is with you?" Dread fills my stomach.

"No," I breathe as I stand up and head to the front door. "N-No, Nona, she left a while ago." I open the door to the blanket of Hell that has dropped on my driveway since I fell asleep.

"Grant, she never got back and I can't get her to answer the phone." I hear the sob she's trying to hold back.

"I'll find her," I say as I grab my boots. "I'll find her, Nona, I'll call you back." Hanging up, I lace my boots and am about to shut the door when Holly walks over.

"I'll find her," I say, though at this point I think I'm just trying to reassure myself. I make my way through the snow, while trying my best to stay balanced. Getting in the truck I take a breath while starting the ignition.

"You better be okay."

I make it half way down the hill when brake lights catch my attention. "Oh God." I pull my truck over and get out of the cab while making my way to her stupid, tiny ass loaner that I'm going to shove up someone's ass tomorrow. It looks like she lost control going down the hill and the car hit the ditch. I brush the snow off the window and see her laying over the steering wheel.

"Fuck," I rasp while ripping the door open. "Elsie," I cry out as my hand touches her face. She groans, and it's the sweetest sound I've ever heard. She shifts and whines as she comes to and lifts her head.

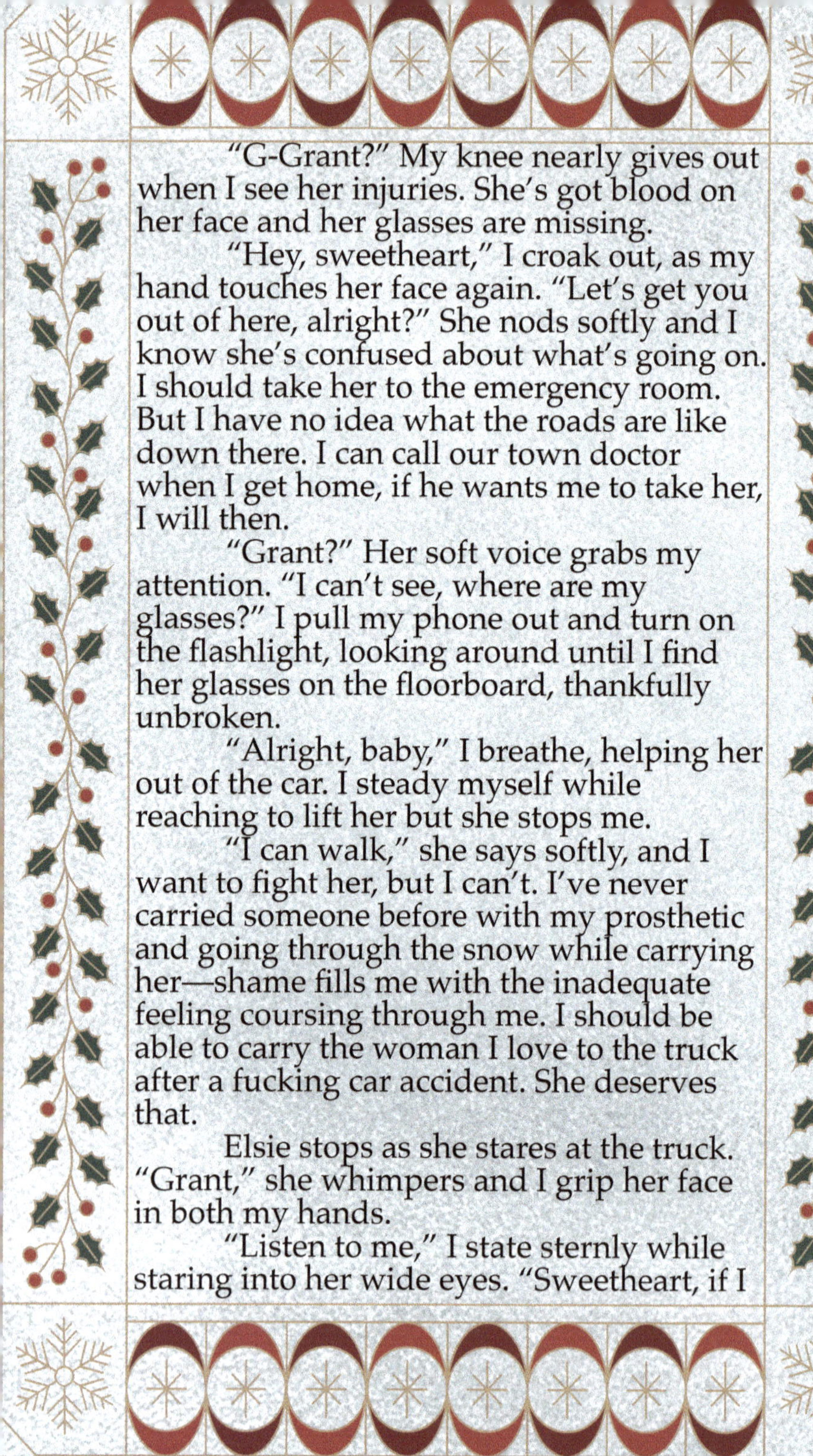

"G-Grant?" My knee nearly gives out when I see her injuries. She's got blood on her face and her glasses are missing.

"Hey, sweetheart," I croak out, as my hand touches her face again. "Let's get you out of here, alright?" She nods softly and I know she's confused about what's going on. I should take her to the emergency room. But I have no idea what the roads are like down there. I can call our town doctor when I get home, if he wants me to take her, I will then.

"Grant?" Her soft voice grabs my attention. "I can't see, where are my glasses?" I pull my phone out and turn on the flashlight, looking around until I find her glasses on the floorboard, thankfully unbroken.

"Alright, baby," I breathe, helping her out of the car. I steady myself while reaching to lift her but she stops me.

"I can walk," she says softly, and I want to fight her, but I can't. I've never carried someone before with my prosthetic and going through the snow while carrying her—shame fills me with the inadequate feeling coursing through me. I should be able to carry the woman I love to the truck after a fucking car accident. She deserves that.

Elsie stops as she stares at the truck. "Grant," she whimpers and I grip her face in both my hands.

"Listen to me," I state sternly while staring into her wide eyes. "Sweetheart, if I could carry you on my back and climb this hill to avoid putting you in that truck, you have to believe me, I would. And I promise you, first chance I get, I'm getting a new truck. But I need you to get in there so I can take you back to my place. Please." Her bottom lip trembles but she nods while hesitantly climbing into the driver's seat and scooting to the middle of the bench seat. "That's my girl, alright." I climb in and shut the door in time for her to climb onto my lap. She straddles me and buries her face into my neck as sobs wrack through her.

"Elsie," I choke out, rubbing her back.

"I was so scared. I couldn't stop and I was so scared that—that you would come down the hill and see me dead, hanging half out of the car, partially frozen."

"Okay, well that is a visual I could've done without," I state slowly as she shifts, and I roll my eyes as I feel her center on my cock. *Not happening. No, no! I will not get a boner while she's sobbing from nearly dying.*

"It's a visual I could've done without, too." She sniffles while pulling back. "I see it every day. I see David, I hear the brakes and the horn. I smell the tires. I see you." Her eyes search mine, for what, I don't know. "Do you ever see any of it?" Her question is so small sounding and I give her a small sigh.

"No, sweetheart, not much. I—I was fading in and out so much. I only

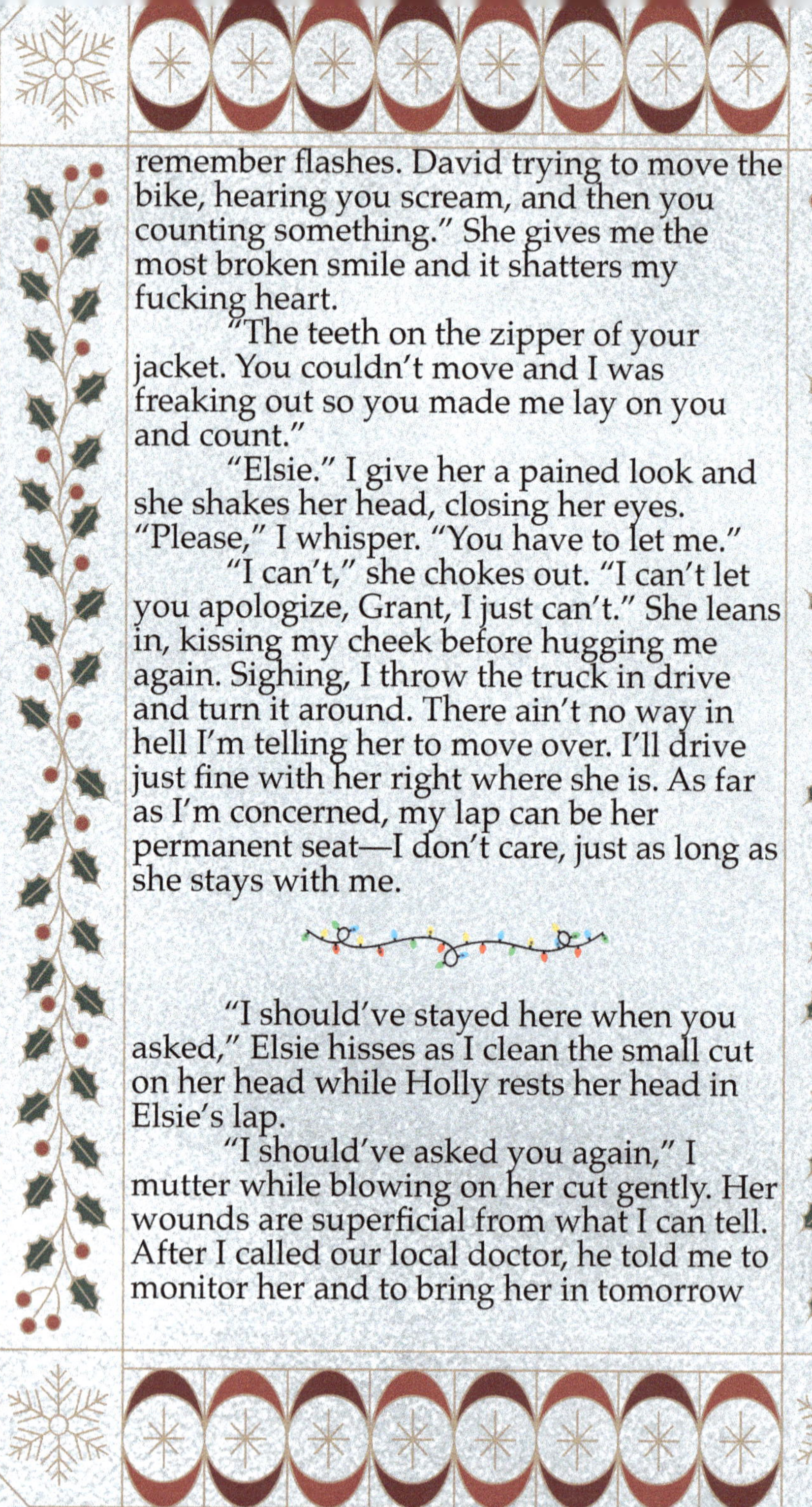

remember flashes. David trying to move the bike, hearing you scream, and then you counting something." She gives me the most broken smile and it shatters my fucking heart.

"The teeth on the zipper of your jacket. You couldn't move and I was freaking out so you made me lay on you and count."

"Elsie." I give her a pained look and she shakes her head, closing her eyes. "Please," I whisper. "You have to let me."

"I can't," she chokes out. "I can't let you apologize, Grant, I just can't." She leans in, kissing my cheek before hugging me again. Sighing, I throw the truck in drive and turn it around. There ain't no way in hell I'm telling her to move over. I'll drive just fine with her right where she is. As far as I'm concerned, my lap can be her permanent seat—I don't care, just as long as she stays with me.

"I should've stayed here when you asked," Elsie hisses as I clean the small cut on her head while Holly rests her head in Elsie's lap.

"I should've asked you again," I mutter while blowing on her cut gently. Her wounds are superficial from what I can tell. After I called our local doctor, he told me to monitor her and to bring her in tomorrow morning for a check-up, but she's coherent and responsive.

"You're always looking for a reason to blame yourself," she murmurs and I can't stop the huff that leaves me as I clean up.

"Not looking, it just seems to happen." Glancing down, my eyes linger over her. She's dressed in my dark gray hoodie and nothing else. I'll never wash that hoodie again I swear to fucking God. I want her smell to be embedded in that cotton permanently.

"Not polite to stare." She gives me a weak, playful smile and I jerk back.

"Sorry, I was—" *Was what, you perverted fuck? Was thinking about how you're going to wrap that hoodie around your face while you jerk off to thoughts of her? Sure, Grant, go on and tell her that.* "Looking for bruises." *Wow, you stupid fucking liar.*

"Uh-huh." She laughs lightly. "It's okay, I stare at you, too." She shrugs and I nearly trip over myself while heading to the kitchen.

"Do—what?"

"What? You're good looking and you have a nice butt. Am I not supposed to appreciate that?"

"Okay, you definitely need to go to the doctor tomorrow," I mutter while trying to hide the smirk pulling at my lips. "You've obviously hit your head harder than I thought."

6

ELSIE

"Right, I understand what you're saying, Ms. Shoemaker." I rub my temples as I listen to the woman continue to yell at me for having to postpone our meeting due to my accident.

"How are you supposed to properly judge my pies if you aren't eating them fresh?" she huffs and I have to fight back a groan. This project was supposed to bring me more holiday cheer and instead, I'm feeling less than ever before. Which, let me tell you, really sucks because it means Grant is right. And while I'm head-over-heels for the man, it doesn't mean I want his stubborn ass getting to say 'I told you so'. No, *I* am the one who

gets to scream that when I fill *him* with the holiday cheer. Grant is *not* filling me with—

Grant comes out of his room and I quickly avert my gaze. He's shirtless and very beautiful with his soft looking skin, dusting of black hair and soft muscles that I want to sink my teeth into. He walks over to me and leans over—causing his masculine, clean scent to invade my senses.

"Ms. Shoemaker!" he says loudly with fake enthusiasm. "Are my ears deceiving me or did I just overhear you yelling at sweet Elsie here about not being able to taste your pies this morning due to her car accident and the large amount of snow we got?"

Ms. Shoemaker exhales loudly. "I just believe it's in poor taste. She's going to try the pies in what? Two, three days, and then make her decision? How is that fair? Pies are best when eaten fresh!"

"Oh, I completely agree, which is why I'm confused about all the emotion coming from your end considering your pies are made from a can. Now, stop calling Elsie. I'll be in touch if we need a replacement." Grant hits the end call button on my phone and stands back up.

"Grant!" I hiss, while staring up at him in shock. "Ms. Shoemaker—"

"Is a fucking bitch. Now stop allowing her to drain you. You told her you were in an accident and stuck due to the snow in the email you sent last night. Stop allowing yourself to be so accessible to these people." I know he's right, but it's so hard, I hate disappointing everyone.

"I was thinking about removing the front vendor's spot," I admit softly, knowing it won't go over well. "I thought about seeing if you could put a couple walls up to block off the area and maybe we could make it like a Santa's workshop. Remember? Like when we were kids? And then maybe a dog adoption area? I don't know, I feel like I need to either give everyone the first spot or no one, ya know?" I look up at him as he considers me for a minute. He frowns before walking into his kitchen.

"How's your head?" he calls back and I roll my eyes. It's been two days since my accident. I'm fine. I'm sore, but fine. Okay, I'm not fine. I've spent the last two nights in the same house as Grant and after riding on his lap and feeling his holy-hell boner—*oh yes, I felt it*. No way I imagined *that* and my god if that's what he's rocking in there… Well, let's just say I thought I was sexually frustrated before, but now I can't stop looking at him like I'm starving and he is a delicious hunk of meat. God, I would take a bite out of him so—

"Are you ignoring me?"

"What!?" I scream at his question as he returns from the kitchen. He stands by the table with a confused expression as I clutch my chest and my face goes red. "Sorry," I whisper. "I was… in thought."

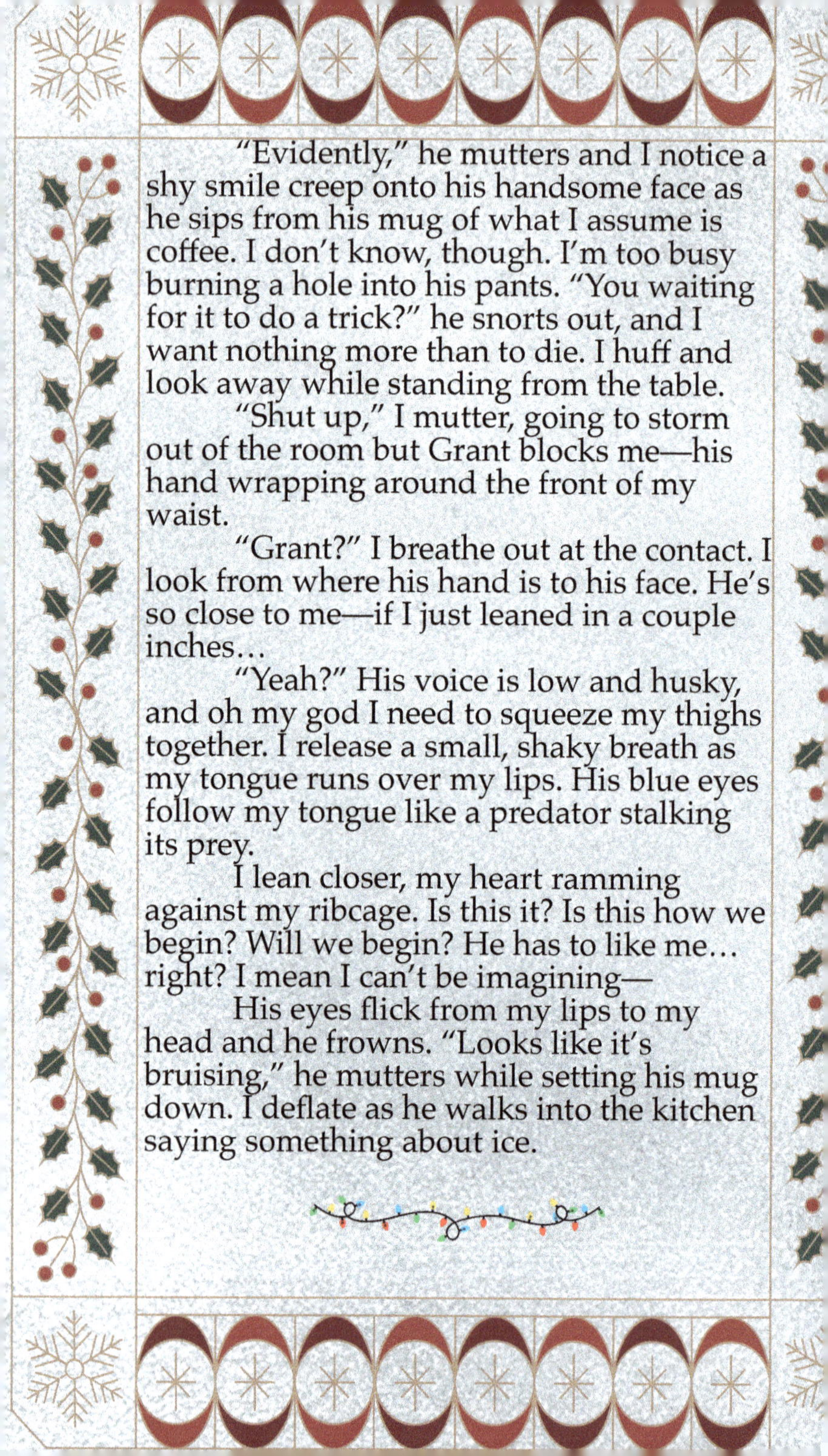

"Evidently," he mutters and I notice a shy smile creep onto his handsome face as he sips from his mug of what I assume is coffee. I don't know, though. I'm too busy burning a hole into his pants. "You waiting for it to do a trick?" he snorts out, and I want nothing more than to die. I huff and look away while standing from the table.

"Shut up," I mutter, going to storm out of the room but Grant blocks me—his hand wrapping around the front of my waist.

"Grant?" I breathe out at the contact. I look from where his hand is to his face. He's so close to me—if I just leaned in a couple inches…

"Yeah?" His voice is low and husky, and oh my god I need to squeeze my thighs together. I release a small, shaky breath as my tongue runs over my lips. His blue eyes follow my tongue like a predator stalking its prey.

I lean closer, my heart ramming against my ribcage. Is this it? Is this how we begin? Will we begin? He has to like me… right? I mean I can't be imagining—

His eyes flick from my lips to my head and he frowns. "Looks like it's bruising," he mutters while setting his mug down. I deflate as he walks into the kitchen saying something about ice.

"Are you trying to kill me?" Nona scolds while slamming her thermos down on my counter with an overly dramatic bang.

"I think there's an argument to be had here that I'm trying to *save* you," I reply dryly as she rears back as if I've slapped her.

"Elsie Penelope Marshall! You think I won't jump over this counter and clock you with this cane? Try me. Now, give me my order and if you sneak that decaf shit in there one more time—"

"Fine!" I groan while dumping out her thermos in the sink and prepare the machine to make her the five shots of espresso she wants mixed in with her light roast. "You're going to have a heart attack drinking all this!"

"Please, if I'm still able to hop in a swing while four men a third my age partake—"

"Oh. My. God!" I scream while covering my ears. "Stop! For the love of God—Stop!" She snickers while waiting for me to finish her coffee.

"Don't be all upset because I have a healthy sex life and you're sitting there whimpering in need."

"You are my *grandmother*!" I huff as I shoved the thermos at her.

"Precisely! I'm worried about you! Listen, if you want…" She lets out a long sigh. "I'm willing to let you have the boys for a weekend, but we must never speak of

it. I don't much like the thought of sharing my partners with my grandchild. But I can't stand to see you hurting." My mouth falls open as I stare at her grinning face.

"You're a loon. Now go to—" *Oh, son of a bitch.* The bell chimes and I look to see Grant walking in to get his daily coffee. Damn it, this is only going to end—

"Grant!" Nona beams brightly at the delicious looking man. God, he has no right being so good looking in work boots and jeans. "I have a favor to ask of you, would you mind helping an old lady out?" I give Grant the 'run' look that he seems to ignore while looking at the old woman.

"Yeah, I got some time," he mutters and *oh, you poor stupid gorgeous man.*

"Perfect!" Nona cheers. "If you go to my condo, I have my sex swing still set up—it's clean I promise. I need you to get it and bring it here for Elsie." Grant blinks, his jaw slack as he stares at the woman and then to me.

"Don't… look at me," I whine, crouching down behind my counter while simultaneously praying an alien will come and abduct me.

Nona grabs the thermos off the counter. "Now, make sure when you grab the swing, you take the one on the door, not the big one. She ain't ready for all that yet, plus I have a date tonight with a couple ladies and I can't cancel on them again." I hear Nona walk out of the shop but I don't dare move from my spot. Screw the aliens, if this floor could just open up and just suck me in, that would be amazing right now.

"Els." Grant sounds about as stunned as I feel.

"Uh-huh?" It comes out almost like a whimper at this point.

"I uhmm… I'm not going to go get your grandmother's sex swi—"

"Of course you're not!" I hiss while popping back up. "Obviously she's just trying to start something!"

"Start what?" he asks cautiously while I turn around and start making his coffee, not bothering to ask him if he wants anything extra. He wants it black, and I'm not feeling like trying to get him to try anything today.

"I have no sex life and she has enough for the whole town. She's trying to get me laid."

"Wow, that's gotta be the weirdest thing I've ever heard," he mutters as I all but shove the drink at him.

"It's Nona," I snip, my cheeks burning from embarrassment. "She won't be happy until I've knocked the cobwebs off my vagin—" Grant's mid-sip as he sputters and coughs at my remark. "Oh please, Mr. Gray Sweatpants." I sigh while handing him a paper towel.

"What the hell is that supposed to mean?" he rasps between coughs while hitting his chest.

"You waiting for it to do a trick?" I state in probably the worst imitation of

him. He is either not amused at all or so amused I've broken his face.

"Boy you're awfully grumpy today," he mutters, sipping his coffee again.

"Can you blame me!?" I cry while waving my hands around in frustration. "My loaner is totaled, and my car is still days from being done. Everyone is being an absolute butthead over this damn market thing. You're walking around with muscles and naked skin. I'm freaking broke and living in the break room. I haven't been invited to partake in a sex swing activity by anyone other than my *grandmother*. I need a thousand dollars, a plate of cheese fries and an orgasm and I'm not seeing any in my future!" I scream while smacking the snowflake I have taped on the cash register off and stepping on it.

"Uh, Grant?" The unfamiliar male voice makes me cringe as I look up and, *who the hell is he?* I want to cry as the large, blond man stands by the door, his dark brown eyes laser-focused on me.

"Dean, go to the market," Grant nearly growls while his eyes pin me. There are far too many sets of eyes on me right now.

"Yeah but I wa—"

"Dean!" Grant barks and Dean leaves the shop.

"Who's Dean?" I whisper while keeping eye contact with Grant.

"New hire."

"Oh, he seems nice." I keep my voice small as Grant walks toward me. He moves around the counter and I back up only to have him follow me until I'm against a wall.

"He's not," he states through gritted teeth, still staring intently at me. I feel my heart rate increasing to an alarming rate.

"That's unfortunate." Why am I still going with this conversation? Why did I tell him I needed cheese fries and an orgasm? I mean, I do. God, I need them both *so* bad. But now Grant knows. And his new hire. Jesus, this is going to be so bad if Dean is working with him at the Christmas Market. "Do you want me to apologize to Dean for my outburst?"

"No."

"No? Then why are you glaring at me?"

"Because you keep saying his name and every time you do, I envision being far more violent than I have any right being." The air whooshes from my lungs as my eyes go wide.

"Grant?" I manage out. I notice his chest is rising and falling faster than normal. "What are you thinking?"

"Things I shouldn't think," he admits with no hesitation as he steps closer into my space, forcing me to crane my neck.

"Tell me." I shudder as his fingertips run up my arm.

"Why?" he mumbles—leaning in so his lips are against my ear. "What good

would it do for you to know that I liked you staring at my cock? That the thought turned me on so much I got off to it in the shower? How will it help you to know that I want to consume you from lips to lips." His finger trails over my lips, down to the front of my pants, causing heat to rush between my legs. "Tell me, Els, how is it going to help you to know that all I can think about right now is how fucking sinful you would look with your mouth falling open as moans escape you while your eyes glaze over in pleasure and roll back in your head as you pant *my* name from that needy little mouth."

"Oh my God," I whimper in need and it causes him to chuckle.

"Grant works just fine, sweetheart." He pulls away from my ear and I stare at him in wonder. Is—does he really have feelings for me, too?

"Fuck it," I whisper, reaching my hands to the collar of his shirt, pulling him into me. Our lips meet and I expect him to freeze, to pull away, but he doesn't. Grant groans as he grips my jaw in one hand and my hair in his other as he devours my mouth.

"Fucking Christ," he whimpers between our kisses.

"Elsie works just fine, sweetheart," I pant and he chuckles lowly before plunging his tongue into my mouth. The whine I release is so needy and I don't care, I am needy. I need Grant even more now than I did forty-five seconds ago.

His large, rough hands pull my tucked shirt from my pants before sliding them over my waist. My hips buck toward him, causing him to moan.

"Els," he groans against my mouth. "Sweetheart, I—"

The doorbell chimes and Grant all but shoves himself away from me as…

"Ms. Shoemaker!" My voice is far too breathy as I say her name. The older pointed woman stares down her slender nose at me, her icy eyes full of judgment.

"Ah, so this is why you've been too busy to talk with me. I have been waiting at the square for you and one of the workers stated you were still here. I didn't realize you were… entertaining." Her wrinkled lips press together in annoyance.

"Ms. Shoemaker, as I stated before—"

"Interesting choice," she interrupts, eyes still burning into Grant. "Going after this one when he's to blame for David." Grant's entire body stiffens and I feel cold all over. "You know, my sweet granddaughter, Beth, still cries over him. Still wears that promise ring. I guess some move on faster than others. Well, have a good day." Ms. Shoemaker spins on her heel and walks out of the shop.

Grant runs his hands over his scruffy face before moving them to the back of his neck and squeezing.

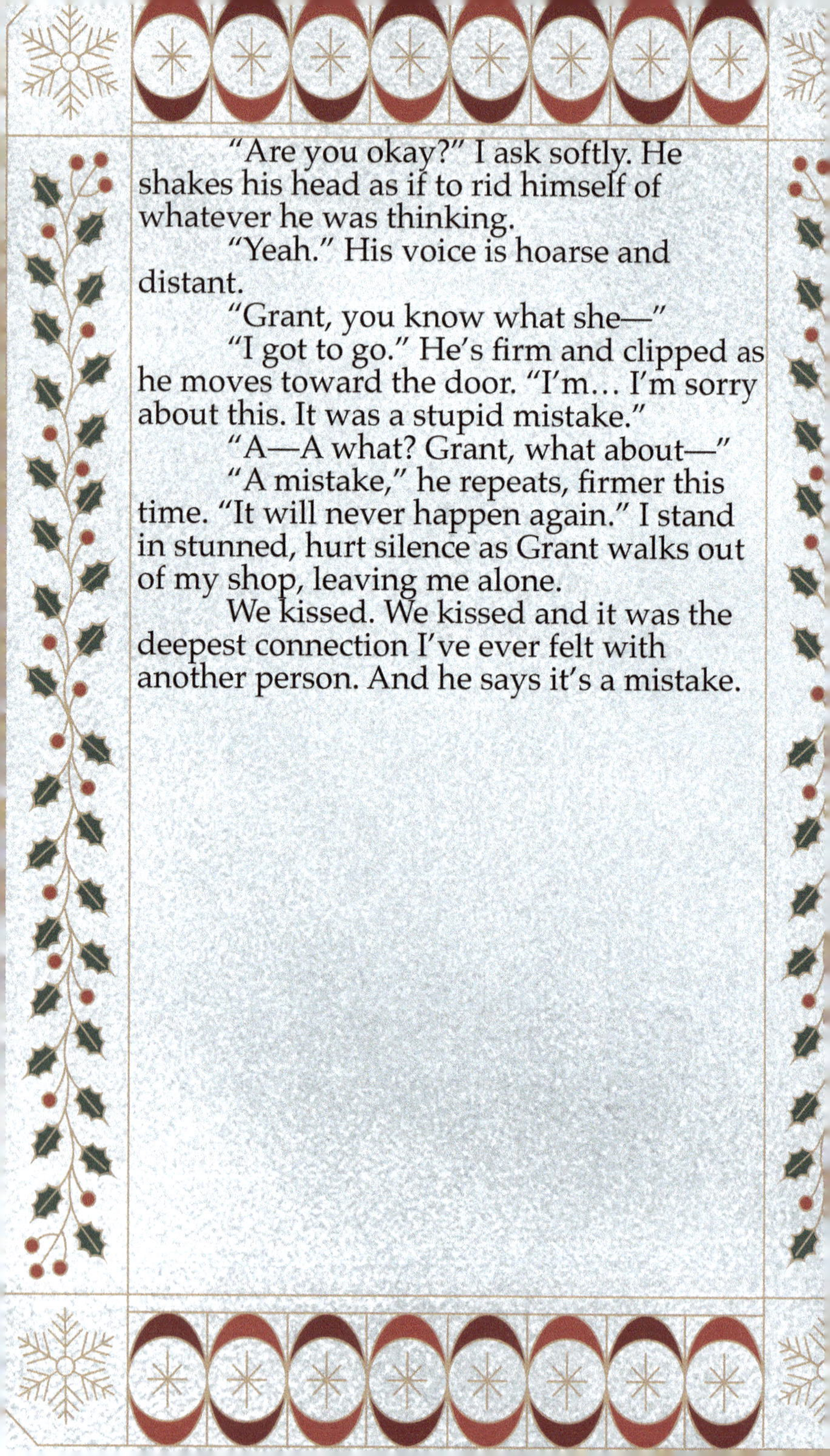

"Are you okay?" I ask softly. He shakes his head as if to rid himself of whatever he was thinking.

"Yeah." His voice is hoarse and distant.

"Grant, you know what she—"

"I got to go." He's firm and clipped as he moves toward the door. "I'm… I'm sorry about this. It was a stupid mistake."

"A—A what? Grant, what about—"

"A mistake," he repeats, firmer this time. "It will never happen again." I stand in stunned, hurt silence as Grant walks out of my shop, leaving me alone.

We kissed. We kissed and it was the deepest connection I've ever felt with another person. And he says it's a mistake.

7

GRANT

I am the dumbest mother fucking son of a bitch to ever exist. I don't know what in the fuck I was thinking. I kissed her. I *kissed* Elsie. And those filthy things I said to her. Jesus Christ, how am I ever supposed to look at her again? When Via Shoemaker walked into the shop and said those things, it brought all of the fears I was trying to ignore back to the forefront.

I am the reason her big brother is dead, I'm the reason Via's granddaughter, Beth, lost her boyfriend and fuck, David loved that woman with everything he had. I'm the cause of so much sadness and I had my tongue down Elsie's throat? I'm so fucking stupid.

I look up from where Holly is sleeping under my makeshift workbench and to Dean, my new carpenter. Dean is supposed to be helping me with construction on the Christmas market. But since Elsie arrived here an hour ago, he's found every excuse to assist her. It's pissing me off. Especially because Elsie is giggling at his flirtatious bullshit. *Giggling.* She's walking around with damp underwear because of *me* and she's giggling at him?

You're the one that called it a mistake, asshole. Knock it off.

"Dean!" I bark out, startling the blond man. "I ain't paying you to get a date, now get over here." Elsie glares at me before storming off as Dean walks over—a sheepish grin on his face.

"Sorry, Grant." He laughs lightly. "Ellie is just—" He lets out a breath and I catch his eyes drifting over to where Elsie is hanging some decorations around Santa's chair. "She's great, she's really pretty and funny."

I know she's really pretty and funny. I don't need this fuck that's known her three seconds to tell me what I've known forever. *Pretty* and *funny* are the least descriptive words you could use for her.

"She's also unavailable," I grunt while roughly shoving an impact at him. "Now go hang that temporary wall."

"Wait, she's unavailable? Like she's not wanting to date or she's with someone? Because from what I heard in the shop earlier ah—" I snatch Dean by his shirt collar and force him to face me while ignoring the scream in my leg.

"If you value your life, I would forget everything you heard in the coffee shop, are we understood?"

"Grant!" Elsie hisses while grabbing me by the ear and twisting while walking away.

"Ow! Ow! Ow! Ow!" I yell while swatting her iron-lock grip off my ear. "What the fuck!" I whine while glaring at her.

"You don't get to scare off interested men in my life anymore. I'm not a teenager," she warns and I raise a brow. There's no way she heard me. As if reading my mind, she rolls her eyes. "You're manhandling Dean. You and David did the same shit when we were younger. Stop being a jerk."

"I'm not being a jerk," I grit out. "I'm not paying him to get into your pants." Okay, obviously I could've used better wording, but here we are.

"You don't get to tell me that what happened in the coffee shop is a mistake and then turn around and snarl at any man who looks my way."

"Oh?" I huff out a dry laugh. "You sure about that? Tell me, sweetheart, were you planning on going out with Dean tonight when those soaked panties belong to me?" She opens her mouth to say

something but a squeak comes out as her cheeks flame red.

"I'm your mistake, Grant." Her words are a punch to the gut. "If all you see when you look at me is regret—is a mistake…" My heart aches at the crack in her voice as she speaks. She shakes her head and looks away. "Well, if that's all you see then you need to look elsewhere. I am no one's regretful night, and I'm not a mistake."

"Elsie, it's not that fucking easy and you know it!" I hiss softly as to not draw attention.

"It is, though." She furiously wipes away the tear sliding down her cheek. "I have feelings for you, Grant! And you are playing with me! Stop it because it fucking hurts!" She shoves me away, leaving me stunned at her words.

"Stop looking at me like that," I grumble to Holly from my place on the couch. Holly has been staring at me and huffing since we got home and she realized Elsie wasn't going to be here as well.

A mistake. God, I'm such a piece of shit. Who says that to someone? Let alone someone like Elsie. The last thing she is, is a mistake. *I am the mistake. She* is the one making a mistake with me. I have to hold her back from me. I have to put her back at arm's length where she's been for so long

because of what happened at the coffee shop and my jealousy creeping out with Dean—it's too much. She deserves a fuckwit like Dean. Some stupid moron with no baggage. Someone she doesn't have to look at and see as the cause of her brother's death.

"Do you ever see any of it?"

Her question from the other night when she wrecked is still playing over in my head. I didn't see David get hit, I was spared that nightmare for whatever reason. What I did get though…

"DAVID! NO!"

"Fuck," I grunt while trying to blink away my tears. Holly comes to me and rests her head on my lap and I break.

"I'm sorry," I whisper into the empty house. "Brother, I—I am so sorry. I'm sorry for that night, I'm sorry for Beth, I'm sorry for Nona and Els. Fuck, I'm so sorry for Els." I close my eyes and rest my head back as my hand absently rubs Holly's head and thoughts I'd rather not have start flooding into my head.

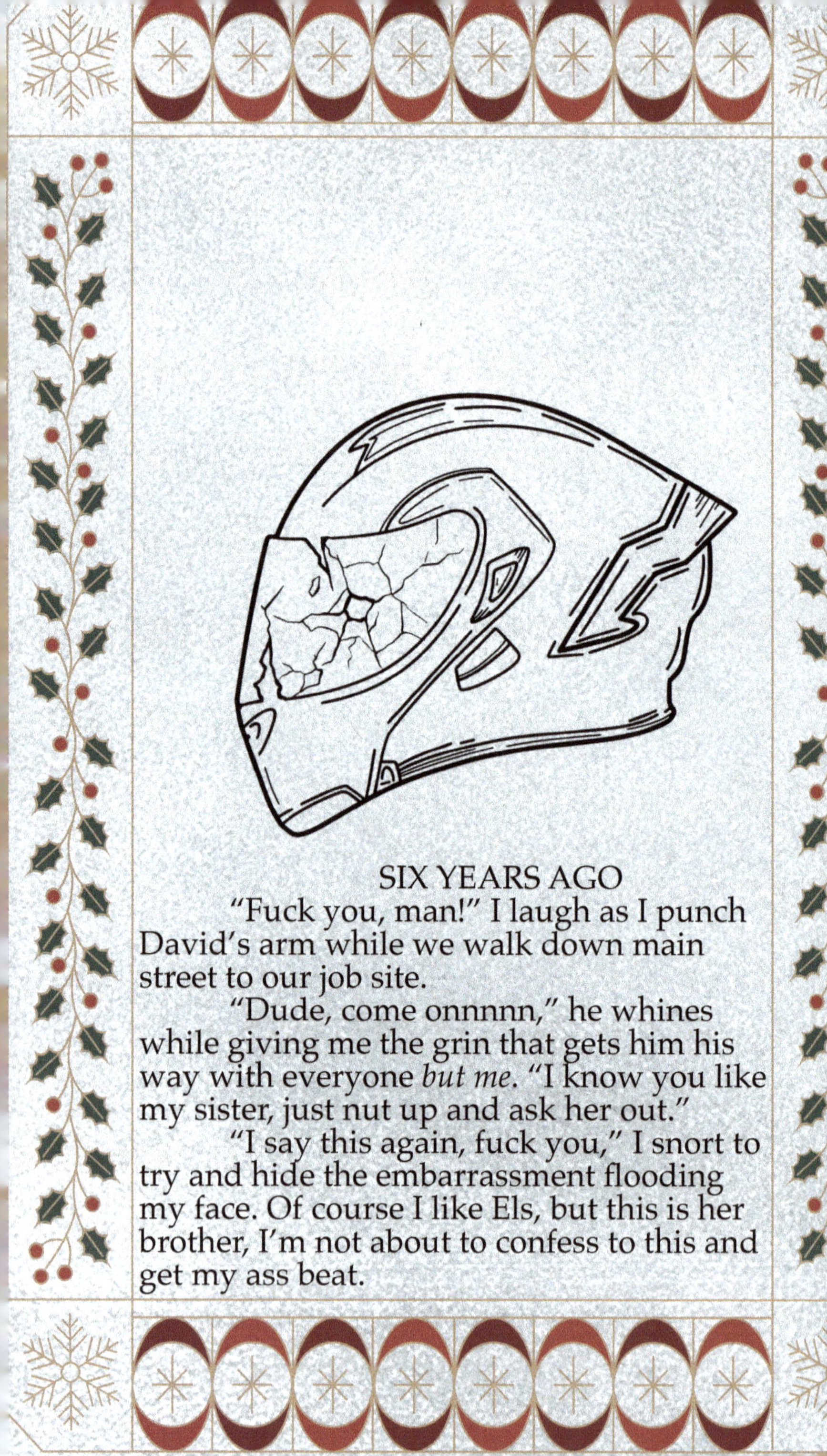

SIX YEARS AGO

"Fuck you, man!" I laugh as I punch David's arm while we walk down main street to our job site.

"Dude, come onnnnn," he whines while giving me the grin that gets him his way with everyone *but me*. "I know you like my sister, just nut up and ask her out."

"I say this again, fuck you," I snort to try and hide the embarrassment flooding my face. Of course I like Els, but this is her brother, I'm not about to confess to this and get my ass beat.

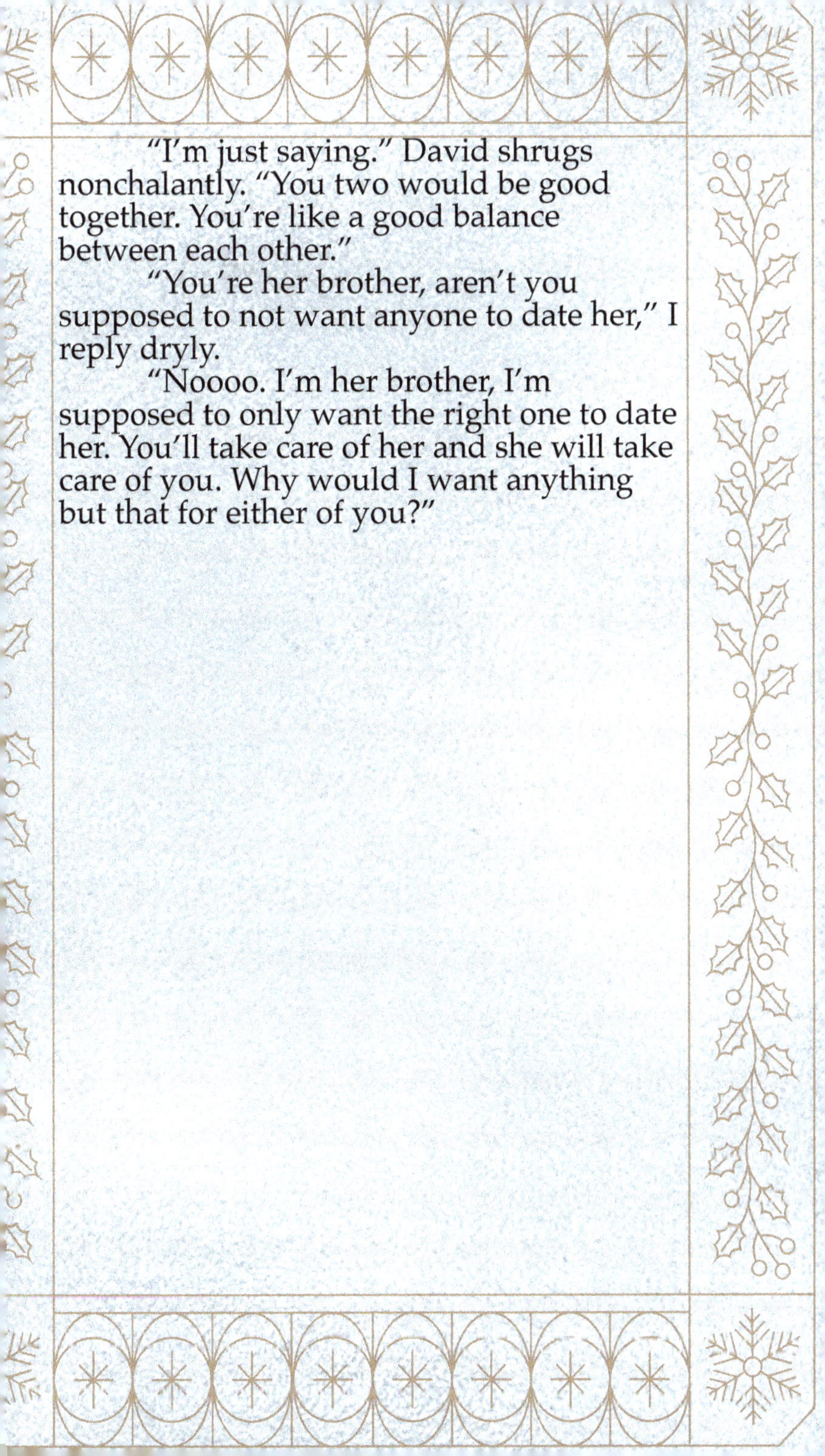

"I'm just saying." David shrugs nonchalantly. "You two would be good together. You're like a good balance between each other."

"You're her brother, aren't you supposed to not want anyone to date her," I reply dryly.

"Noooo. I'm her brother, I'm supposed to only want the right one to date her. You'll take care of her and she will take care of you. Why would I want anything but that for either of you?"

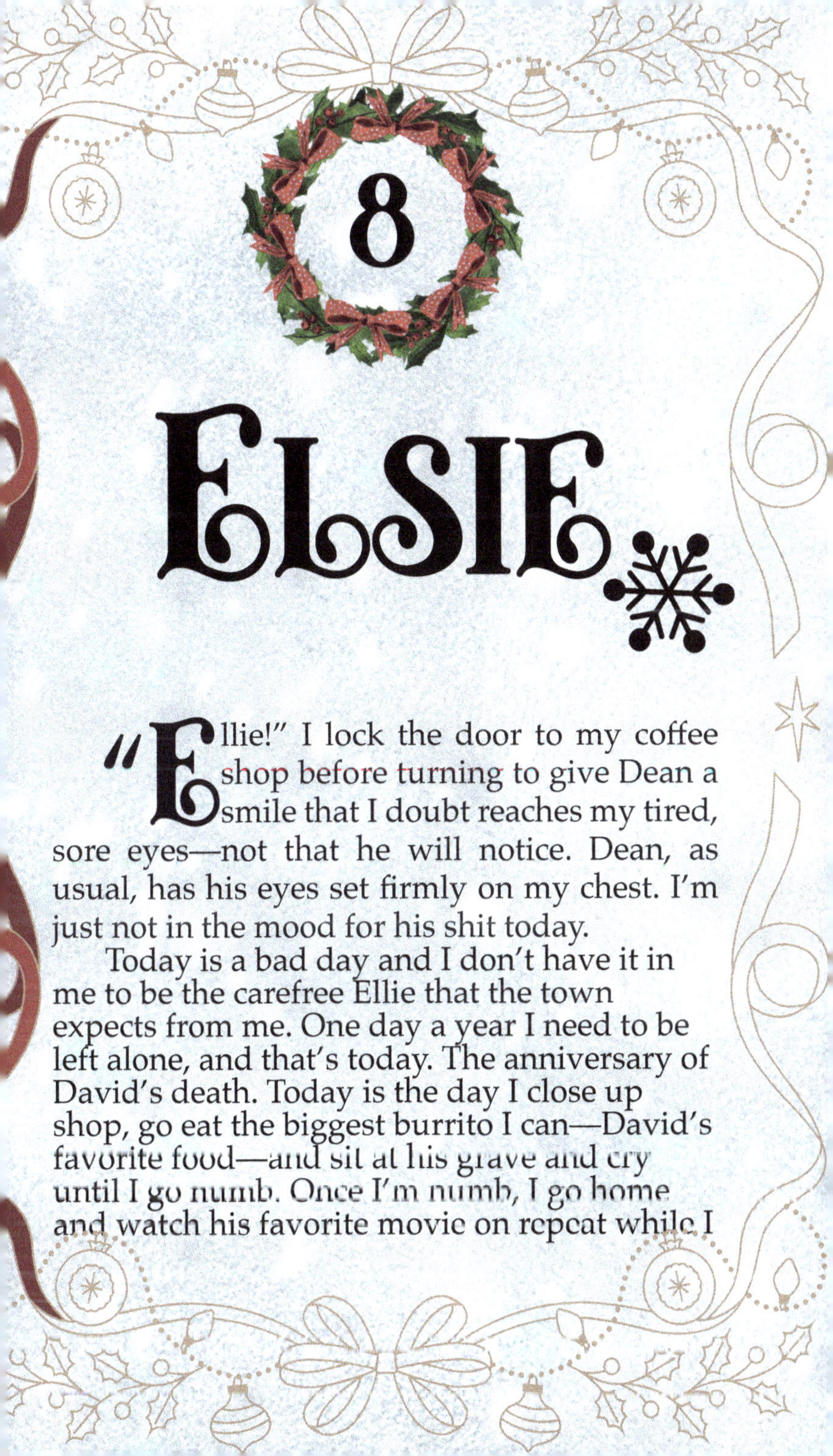

8

ELSIE

"**E**llie!" I lock the door to my coffee shop before turning to give Dean a smile that I doubt reaches my tired, sore eyes—not that he will notice. Dean, as usual, has his eyes set firmly on my chest. I'm just not in the mood for his shit today.

Today is a bad day and I don't have it in me to be the carefree Ellie that the town expects from me. One day a year I need to be left alone, and that's today. The anniversary of David's death. Today is the day I close up shop, go eat the biggest burrito I can—David's favorite food—and sit at his grave and cry until I go numb. Once I'm numb, I go home and watch his favorite movie on repeat while I try to force all the feelings out before I have to put my happy mask back on.

"Hey, Dean," I say softly while stuffing my cold hands in my pockets. "Shop's closed today, sorry."

"Oh no, actually I'm not a big fan of the coffee you have." He laughs lightly. "I think I just prefer my own at home." *You're supposed to give him a light laugh and smile, Elsie.*

"Oh." I crack on the laugh. "Well, sorry about that." Dean's face falls.

"What? No, it was a joke. I'm sorry, it didn't deliver right. Fuck." He rubs the back of his head and I close my eyes and inhale deeply while placing the mask back on even though I would rather die.

"No! Sorry, I'm a little scattered today!" I giggle as I force the brightness in my eyes and voice that is expected of me. "So, what can I do for you?"

"I wanted to see if you wanted to grab some lunch?" *Oh God, a date.*

"Oh," I trail off and wince at the rejection on his face. "Uhm… Yeah sure– okay! What were you thinking?"

"I know a place that makes killer loaded cheese fries." *Cheese fries.* Oh my God… Cheese fries and an orgasm. This is so embarrassing.

Giving him an uncomfortable smile, I shrug slightly as my hands squeeze around something in my coat pocket. "Uh, sure," I say softly while pulling the items out. Gloves. Grant's gloves.

"Awesome! Come on, my car is across the street." I look at the gloves again before stuffing them back into my pocket and forcing a smile despite wanting to cry.

I should just tell him no. I don't want to go out with him today, tomorrow or ever. But all I can think about is Grant telling me it was a mistake to kiss me. That *we* are a mistake. I don't want to feel like a mistake anymore, I want to be someone's choice.

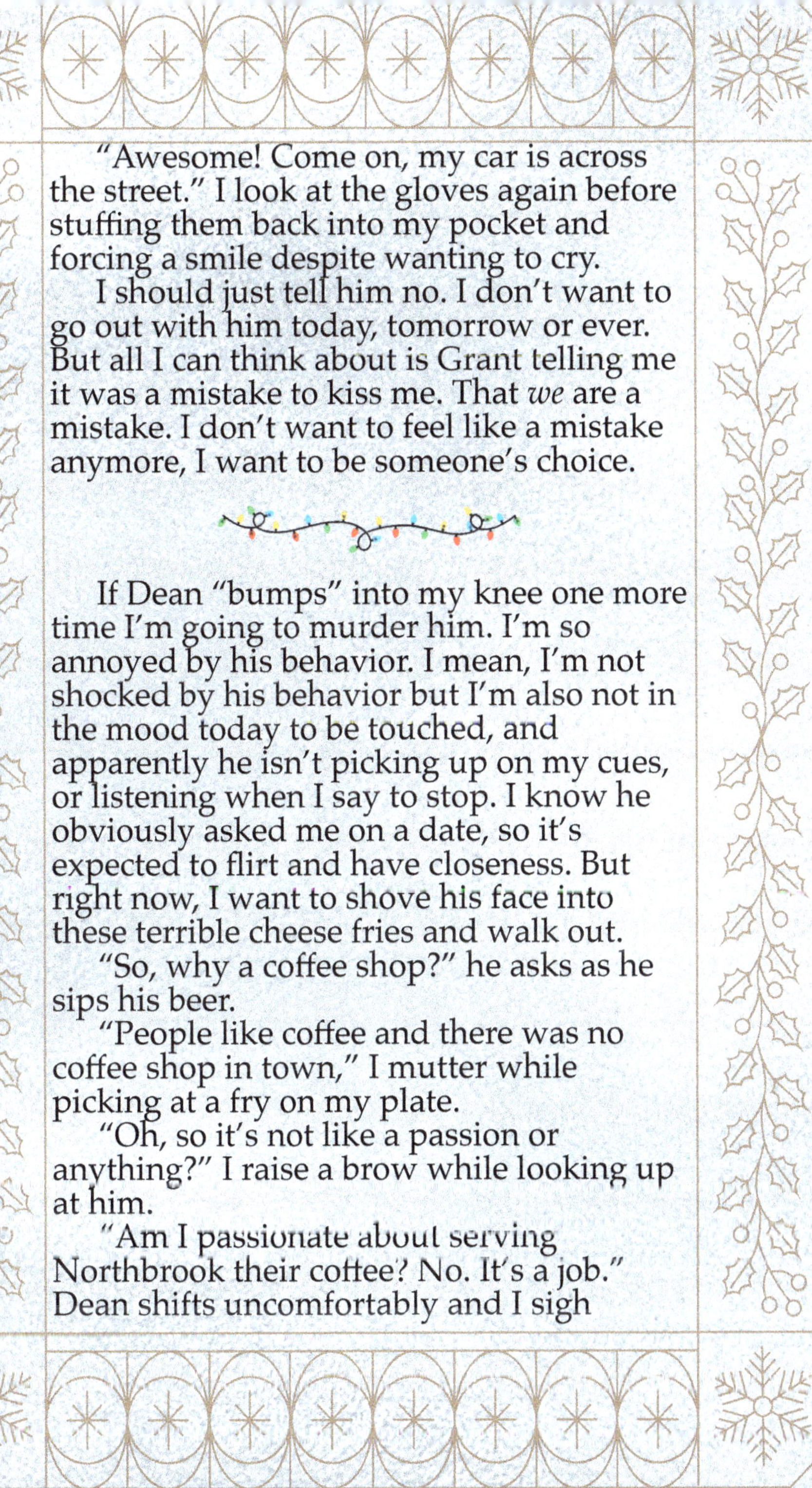

If Dean "bumps" into my knee one more time I'm going to murder him. I'm so annoyed by his behavior. I mean, I'm not shocked by his behavior but I'm also not in the mood today to be touched, and apparently he isn't picking up on my cues, or listening when I say to stop. I know he obviously asked me on a date, so it's expected to flirt and have closeness. But right now, I want to shove his face into these terrible cheese fries and walk out.

"So, why a coffee shop?" he asks as he sips his beer.

"People like coffee and there was no coffee shop in town," I mutter while picking at a fry on my plate.

"Oh, so it's not like a passion or anything?" I raise a brow while looking up at him.

"Am I passionate about serving Northbrook their coffee? No. It's a job." Dean shifts uncomfortably and I sigh loudly. "I'm sorry," I whisper. "It's a bad day. You don't deserve my wrath."

Dean seems to relax and gives me an easy smile. "I'm sorry you're having a bad day, you wanna talk about it?" I wrinkle my nose and shake my head.

"Long story short, it's the anniversary of my brother's passing." He gives me a small nod while sipping his beer again.

"I'm sorry, yeah, I can understand why you wouldn't be in the best mood." A small smirk creeps onto his face and I feel a firm hand on my knee. "Maybe I could take your mind off of it?" he says suggestively and I rear back. Is he serious?

"Are you… propositioning me after I told you it's the anniversary of my brother's death?"

Dean shrugs as he leans back and takes another drink of beer. "It's not like he died today. It's been a year? Two?"

"Six," I snap and he chuckles.

"Six years and it's still bad enough that you're this broken? Have you tried therapy or something?" I stare down at my drink while trying to hold back a shitty remark.

"Been there for six years," I mutter and Dean laughs.

"Maybe a new therapist or some anti-depressants. I mean, you can't just live in the past."

"So, because I don't want to fuck you I must be living in the past? I'm grieving my brother, you know nothing about him, or me. God, this was such a mistake," I growl while standing up to leave.

"Yeah, I'll say. Jesus, I've never worked so hard for a fuck in my life. I've been flirting with you for days now and I take you out to eat and, what? Your brother died *six years* ago and it's still too soon? I mean, you're cute and all but there's no way you're worth all this drama. Limpin' Grant can have you." I feel prickles on the back of my neck as I glare at Dean while he stands up.

"What did you call him?" I say slowly as I feel my rage reach a dangerous level.

"Limpin' Grant. Because of his peg le—" There's a high-pitched whine and my world goes bright white, causing everyone and everything to disappear. I can tolerate a lot. You can take cracks at me, take advantage of my kindness—whatever, I'll allow it. But *no one* talks bad about Grant in my presence. Absolutely fucking no one.

9

GRANT

Whipping into the parking lot of the bar and grill, I groan when I notice the police cruisers parked out front. "The 5-0?" Nona snorts. "Really? What could she have possibly done? Sing Christmas carols too loudly?" I shrug as she and I make our way toward the entrance. I was at the market working on laying the temporary floor down for Santa's area when Nona called me, screaming that this restaurant was holding Elsie hostage and we had to come get her. I still have no idea what she's talking about but as we walk in and I see Elsie sitting on a bench in handcuffs while Dean talks to an officer—I about lose my fucking shit.

"Elsie." I walk over to the girl who is in near tears.

"Sir, you can't—" Nona interrupts the officer.

"Care to explain why my granddaughter is in handcuffs, Louis? And do so quickly before I call your mother." With Nona handling the cops, I focus all my attention on Elsie. Kneeling down in front of her nervous form, I rest my hand on her thigh, giving it a soft squeeze to get her attention.

"Sweetheart, what happened?" I ask as softly as possible. Her lip quivers as her watery gaze meets mine.

"I'm sorry," she croaks. "It's not a good day and he touched my leg and asked about sex and—"

"Excuse me a second, baby." I kiss her forehead as I stand and turn—storming over to Dean and another cop. I brush by the officer and grab Dean by his shirt collar, slamming him against the wall.

"Grant!" I hear Thomas, the cop, bark my name but I ignore him. I beat his ass in high school, and I'll beat him again if he tries to intervene right now.

"Did you touch her, Dean?" I hiss out, causing the man to wince. "You trying to get your dick wet in *my* girl?"

"G-Grant, I'm sorry! I didn't know she was…"

"Grant!" Elsie's voice pierces through my rage and I turn to her. She gives me a pleading look and… *come on Els, baby, don't look at me like that.* Unable to stand the look of fear on her pretty face—I let out an annoyed sigh before dropping the large man.

"You done being a bitch?" I ask the man who nods frantically. Turning to Thomas, I raise a brow. "Uncuff her,"

"Now, listen here—"

"Un… cuff… her," I growl out while moving into his space. Thomas looks to Louis who mutters something before uncuffing Elsie.

"You all are banned from this establishment," Thomas grunts and I roll my eyes.

"We'll try to survive. Come on, Els." I wrap an arm around her shoulders as Nona and I guide her out of the restaurant. We get to the truck and Elsie stops walking. I go to ask what's wrong, but I know—the truck.

"Wait, wait," I say calmly as Elsie starts shaking her head and backing away.

"I can't do this," she whispers as her fingers start tapping against her thumb. "I can't do this, I can't keep smiling."

Nona grabs the girl's face and pulls Els to meet her gaze. "You stop smiling. You stop with that mask, you hear me?" Elsie shakes her head and I feel the guilt in my chest. Looking around, my eyes land on the building across the street and a plan begins to form in my head. This will either be a great idea or a terrible one but, it's better than her having a panic attack in this parking lot.

"Come on," I tell the ladies while walking towards the building with the name: *Breakthrough*.

"This is a bad idea," Elsie says timidly while slipping the coveralls over her clothes. Nona sits in the chair by the window that looks into the rage room.

"I think this will be good, for both of you," she states firmly while crossing her arms. "Get in there and break some shit."

Walking into a rage room feels like stepping into a controlled storm. The space is dimly lit—brightly industrial, depending on what you want to call the *vibe*. Its walls are reinforced and splattered with remnants of past sessions—cracks in the drywall or faint streaks of paint are everywhere. The air carries a faint metallic tang, a mix of adrenaline and the pieces of shattered objects.

We're greeted by shelves and piles of breakable items: old TVs, glass bottles, plates, and printers. Our gloves, helmets, and face shields lay on a table for us, along with a selection of weapons: bats, crowbars, and sledgehammers. I grab a crowbar and hand it to Els while pulling her face shield down.

"Grant," she whispers nervously. "I really… I don't want to."

"Why?" I ask while grabbing a glass bottle and looking at it. "Are you afraid you'll get hurt? Because you won't, I promise. You know I'd never do something to hurt you."

"No." She winces as I throw the bottle and it hits the wall, shattering. "You… You know I don't want to be that way." *That way.* She means like her abusive father. I soften my gaze as I pat her shoulder.

"You aren't your dad, Els. You never could be. I will tell you, though, that keeping this shit inside—holding back and not owning that grief, it's going to hurt you in the long run." She gives me a sarcastic huff.

"You're one to talk."

"I am," I state firmly. "Look at what I've allowed myself to become. Who I've become. All because I held on to that shit. You're too good, Elsie, don't let it eat you. Don't allow this pain to close you off from everyone. Don't become me." She stares at me for a long moment before timidly walking over to the flat screen and tapping it lightly with the crowbar.

"I'm so angry," she growls out as she taps the television a little harder. I lean back to rest against the wall opposite her, trying to allow her to have this moment. "I'm angry at the driver, I'm angry at you, I'm angry at myself," she says to David and my heart breaks.

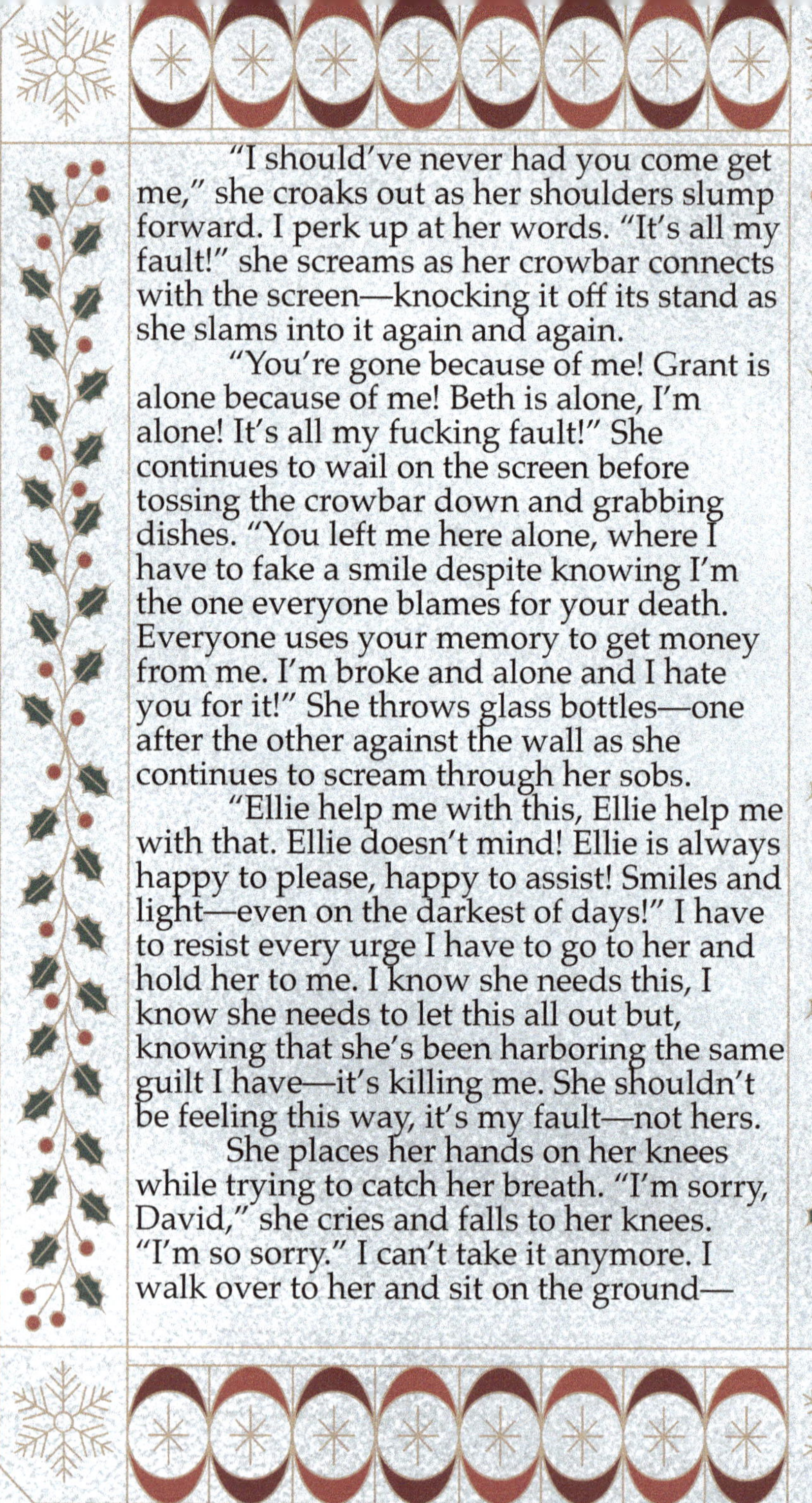

"I should've never had you come get me," she croaks out as her shoulders slump forward. I perk up at her words. "It's all my fault!" she screams as her crowbar connects with the screen—knocking it off its stand as she slams into it again and again.

"You're gone because of me! Grant is alone because of me! Beth is alone, I'm alone! It's all my fucking fault!" She continues to wail on the screen before tossing the crowbar down and grabbing dishes. "You left me here alone, where I have to fake a smile despite knowing I'm the one everyone blames for your death. Everyone uses your memory to get money from me. I'm broke and alone and I hate you for it!" She throws glass bottles—one after the other against the wall as she continues to scream through her sobs.

"Ellie help me with this, Ellie help me with that. Ellie doesn't mind! Ellie is always happy to please, happy to assist! Smiles and light—even on the darkest of days!" I have to resist every urge I have to go to her and hold her to me. I know she needs this, I know she needs to let this all out but, knowing that she's been harboring the same guilt I have—it's killing me. She shouldn't be feeling this way, it's my fault—not hers.

She places her hands on her knees while trying to catch her breath. "I'm sorry, David," she cries and falls to her knees. "I'm so sorry." I can't take it anymore. I walk over to her and sit on the ground—

pulling her into my arms as I remove our shields and eyewear.

"It's not your fault," I choke out, gripping her sobbing body to me as tight as I can—terrified she'll disappear if I let go. "Sweetheart, it wasn't your fault."

"He was picking me up!" she wails into my coveralls. "Had I not called—"

"He died trying to save me," I grit out while forcing her to look at me. "This is *my* fault Elsie. I am the one you should be blaming." Her brows furrow as she shakes her head.

"Grant, no. I will never blame you," she whispers and I roll my eyes.

"Well, that's ridiculous."

"No, what's ridiculous is you thinking you are the cause of this."

"He stopped because of me!" I snap while the guilt and shame begins to fill me. "Had he not seen me—"

"He didn't see you!" she snaps back and I look at her in confusion. "Grant, I saw you, not David. I am the one that told him we needed to stop and check. He didn't see your motorcycle, we almost drove by." I've forgotten how to breathe as I stare at her and I no longer know what I'm feeling. It's almost as if it's anger or betrayal, and it's toward her.

"You told him to stop," I repeat slowly and she nods.

"Yes, and I already see it written on your face so let me answer that question.

Yes, even knowing the outcome—I would tell him to stop again."

"You would tell him to stop—knowing it would kill him. Knowing the pain it would cause you, Nona, the whole fucking town. You would do that all over again—why?" It makes no sense, why would she do that?

"Because it was you," she says simply. "You would've died."

"So?" I huff while shaking my head. "So the fuck what? He would still be alive!" I try to move her away from me so I can stand but she slaps my hands and forces herself on my lap.

"Elsie," I bark, trying to push her back. "Get off!"

"No!" she snaps while grabbing my face—forcing me to look into her red-rimmed eyes. "Your life is valuable, Grant. I need you to understand that I'm not mad over him trying to save you."

"You should be," I growl, looking away. "I'm the reason your brother is dead. It should've been me."

"And I would've still been broken-hearted!" she yells, forcing my gaze back to hers.

"You would've gotten over it," I huff while resting my head against the wall.

"If you think for one second I wouldn't mourn you as much as David, then you are a fool, Grant Anders."

"Why would you? I'm not your brother." I search her eyes as she glares at me.

"No, Grant, you're not my brother. But that doesn't mean I don't care about you, that I don't love you. Do not hurt me by acting as though you don't know how I feel about you." My heart rate quickens at her words and I try to shake my head—to tell her she's foolish. But she doesn't let me.

"And don't insult me by saying I'm wrong. I'm an adult, Grant, I know what I've felt for you for a long time. You don't have to feel the same about me." She sounds almost defeated. "But you don't get to tell me how I should feel about you."

"Goddammit, Elsie," I choke out as she presses her cheek against mine. I wrap my arms around her as tightly as I can while I bury my head into the crook of her neck, inhaling her floral and honey-like scent. I'm not good enough for her. I'm not good enough because she never saw a need to forgive me for David, but all I can think when I see myself is I'm here and he's not. He doesn't get to hold the love of his life in his arms, so why should I?

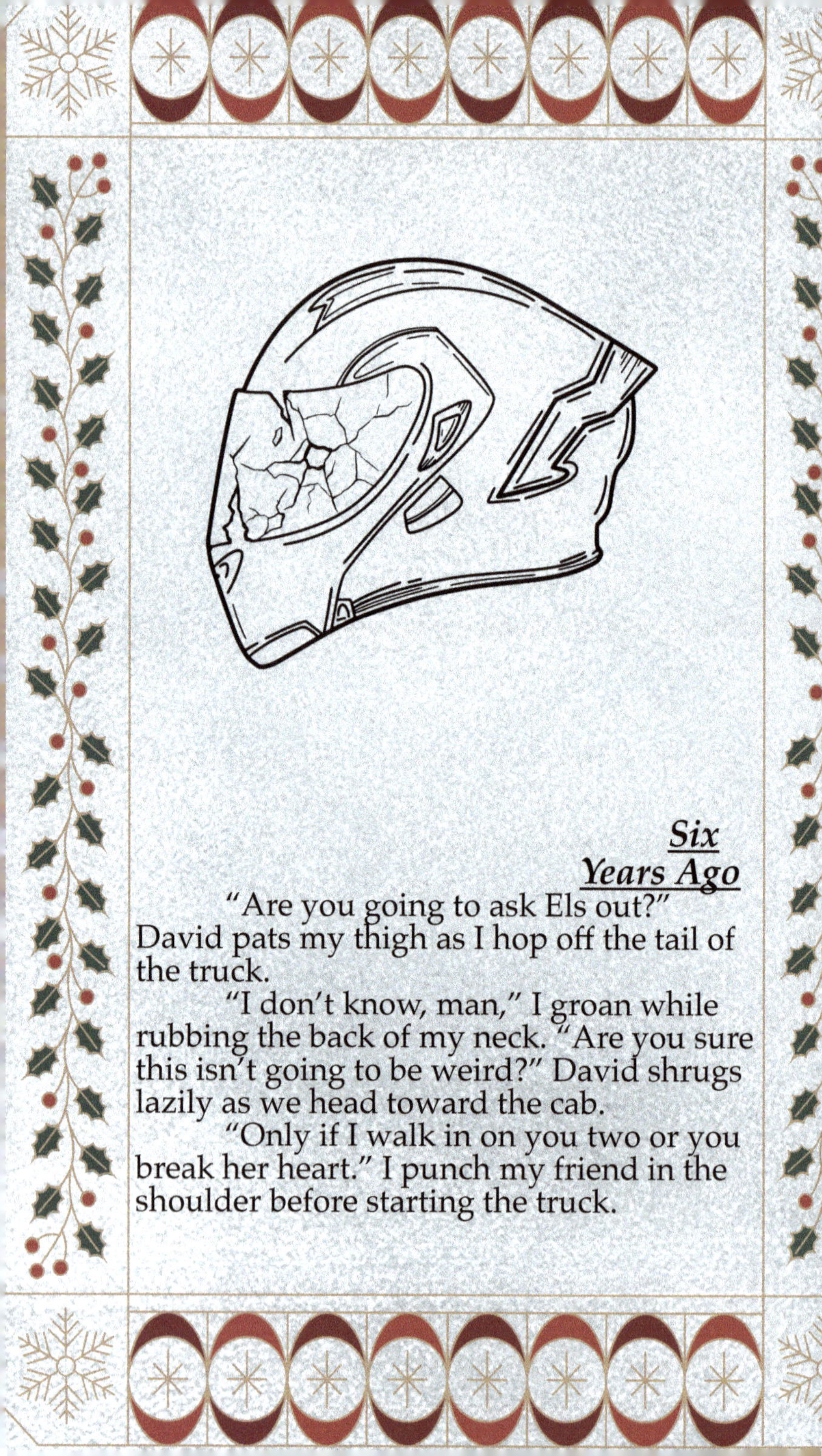

"Are you going to ask Els out?" David pats my thigh as I hop off the tail of the truck.

"I don't know, man," I groan while rubbing the back of my neck. "Are you sure this isn't going to be weird?" David shrugs lazily as we head toward the cab.

"Only if I walk in on you two or you break her heart." I punch my friend in the shoulder before starting the truck.

"I was thinking about asking her to go ice skating tomorrow," I mutter while avoiding his gaze as my cheeks heat up.

"Oh, perfect!" David chuckles. "Put my clumsy sister on ice skates! Seriously, I think you two will have fun. This will be good for you two. You need to admit that you're crazy about each other. She's out at some party tonight so you'll probably need to bring her a hangover cure in the morning."

"Maybe you and Beth could go, too?" I say nervously while trying not to talk myself out of asking Els, again.
"Yeah, sure, I'll ask her tonight. I'll be over at her place unless I've got to pick Elsie's lightweight-ass up tonight."

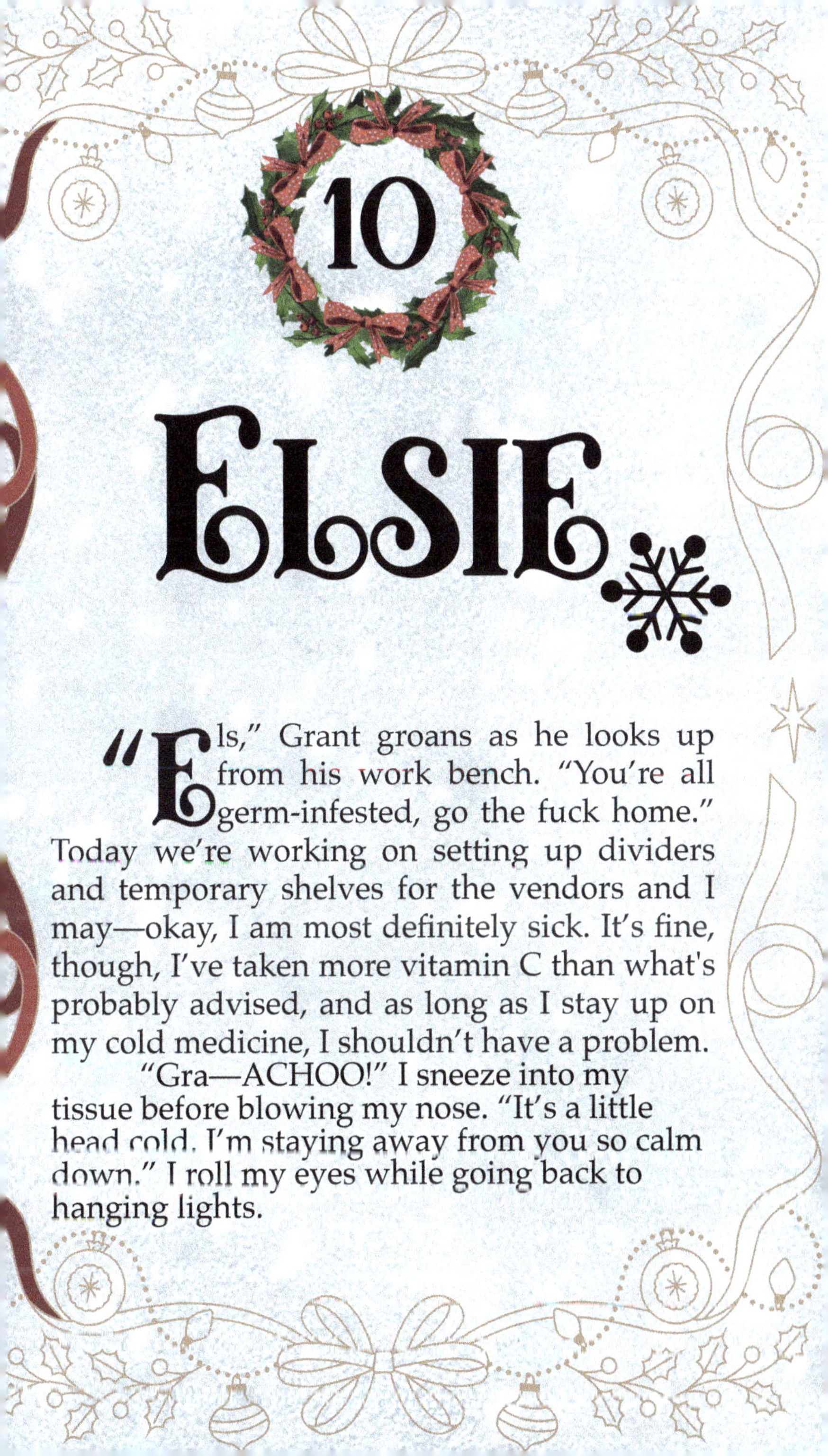

10

ELSIE

"Els," Grant groans as he looks up from his work bench. "You're all germ-infested, go the fuck home." Today we're working on setting up dividers and temporary shelves for the vendors and I may—okay, I am most definitely sick. It's fine, though, I've taken more vitamin C than what's probably advised, and as long as I stay up on my cold medicine, I shouldn't have a problem.

"Gra—ACHOO!" I sneeze into my tissue before blowing my nose. "It's a little head cold. I'm staying away from you so calm down." I roll my eyes while going back to hanging lights.

"Sweet girl, if you think I'm afraid of getting sick, I'll come over there and lick your palm." I shouldn't find that hot, I *really* shouldn't. "I want you to go home and lay the fuck down. You shouldn't be working if you're sick."

"Well I can't, okay," I huff in annoyance. "Someone alerted Betty Rhodes that I'm living in the coffee shop and I was given a warning this morning. Plus there is talk she's going to come here and see how things are going. Apparently some of the vendors have sent her complaints about not being treated well." Sitting on the folding chair, I sigh while blowing my nose again. I notice Grant walking toward me. He's limping pretty bad today and I wonder if he hurt himself in the rage room two days ago. I will admit, getting all of those emotions out felt amazing. But now I'm left with questions. Like what's going to happen between Grant and me? I mean I told him I have feelings for him, but he never responded if he felt the same. And then we didn't see each other yesterday.

"So," he grunts as he shifts his weight off his prosthetic. "Come stay at my house." My eyes threaten to bulge out of my head.

"W—What?" I squeak. "Grant, it was one thing spending the night after the accident but now, I mean, I appreciate it but I have to find an actual place to live." *Which with my current bank account balance is going to be under the Northbrook Bridge.*

"I have the room, it doesn't have to be weird." He shrugs while crossing his arms over his chest.

"Except it would be weird because I would be living with you."

"You mean because of your insatiable lust for me?" He grins as my face goes bright red.

"I—I... You're not being very nice! I'm sick!" I huff as he chuckles.

"Oh, I've be *so* fucking nice. I just offered your pretty ass a free place to stay—no strings attached. You're the one swatting down my offer, not very Christmas spirit of you," he teases and I roll my eyes.

"Yeah, well, bah-humbug." I watch his grin fall and his gaze turns stern.

"Els, what's going on?"

"I already told you. This market has sucked the holiday joy out of my life. I don't even care anymore. I already knew I wasn't going to have a tree and a home to decorate so I wanted to pour it into this and the vendors have ruined it. This feels so... cheap. There's no joy. And now I'm sick on top of it."

"Sweetheart, of course there's no joy. This is the place where the joyless go to capitalize on the holiday. But just wait until the people show up—not the vendors. They'll have all that magical twinkle shit in their eyes and you'll perk up." I force a smile that I don't feel while taking out another tissue and wiping my nose.

"Yeah, you're probably ri—what are you doing?" I ask as Grant grabs my arm and hoists me to my feet.

"Follow me," he says as we head out of the building. I shiver and pull my coat tighter to my body while Grant steps into the snow covered grassy area. I furrow my brows and am about to ask him what he's doing when he turns to face me and falls backward into the snow.

"Oh my God!" I gasp while running to him. "Are you—AH!" I squeal when he reaches for my wrist and yanks me into the snow with him. "Grant! I'm sick! What on—"

"Hush it," he mutters as he moves his arms and legs. Is he—oh my god he's making a snow angel. I watch in bewilderment as he continues to move his arms and legs. After a moment, he stops and a serious look washes over his face.

"What is it?" I ask, while glancing at him.

"How do I get up without leaving a hand or footprint?" I giggle at his question as I start making my own snow angel.

"You don't. There's no such thing as a perfect snow angel, there's always a mark when you get up."

"Except for you, right?" He looks at me and I blink in confusion. "*You* are the perfect snow angel."

"I—" I squeak the word as he scoots closer to me.

"I like you," he whispers against my lips and I feel myself melting into the snow.

"Is this a fever dream?" I murmur, causing him to chuckle lightly.

"No, this is my cheesy attempt at wooing you."

"Oh, I'm woo'd," I say quickly. "You are a successful woo-er."

"Oh am I?" he mumbles, his nose running along my jawline. "Just how successful?" A shiver runs through me that has nothing to do with the snow and everything to do with the man giving me whiplash with his back and forth hot and cold.

"Gra—ACHOO!" I turn away and sneeze into my elbow, breaking whatever spell he seems to be under. Grant stands up and turns to me.

"Come on, Els, if you don't want to stay with me I will put you up in the Inn."

"Grant." I stand up but hold his hand when he tries to let go.

"I like you, too, you know that."

"I do," he whispers, still looking at the snow covered ground. "But I also know you shouldn't, and not just because of your brother, but because I've spent years hating myself so much that—" He grimaces while trying to find the words. "I don't think I'm ever going to be able to look at myself and not feel guilt."

I nod softly. "I understand that feeling." I move closer and wrap my arms

around his tapered waist. "I can't look at myself without feeling guilt either. So here's my idea." His eyes find mine and they look pleading. Like he's begging me to give him the answers. "We don't look at ourselves." I state and he blinks.

"What?"

"We stop looking in the mirror. We'll just look at each other."

He chuckles softly at my suggestion. "Ah, avoidance and denial—"

"Shut up." I roll my eyes. "Let's not act like self-hatred is any healthier." He smiles at me before his eyes flick to something behind me. His grin widens.

"Told you you were the perfect snow angel." He gestures with his head and I turn to see my snow angel with no handprints.

"I want to stay at your house," I say firmly and Grant nods.

"Okay." He looks nervous but there is a light in his eyes, like hope. "Okay, come on, I'll take you there so you can rest."

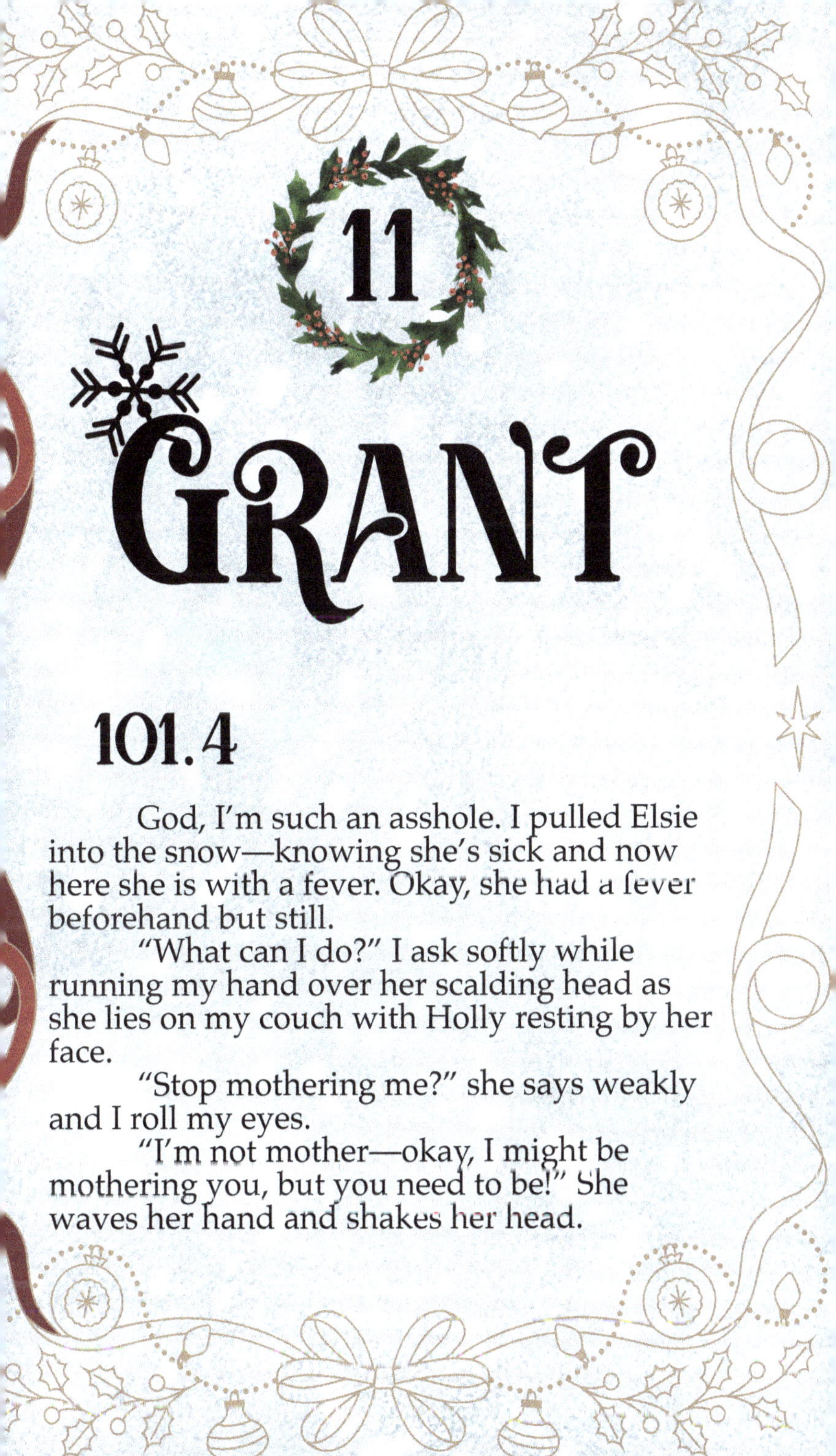

11

GRANT

101.4

God, I'm such an asshole. I pulled Elsie into the snow—knowing she's sick and now here she is with a fever. Okay, she had a fever beforehand but still.

"What can I do?" I ask softly while running my hand over her scalding head as she lies on my couch with Holly resting by her face.

"Stop mothering me?" she says weakly and I roll my eyes.

"I'm not mother—okay, I might be mothering you, but you need to be!" She waves her hand and shakes her head.

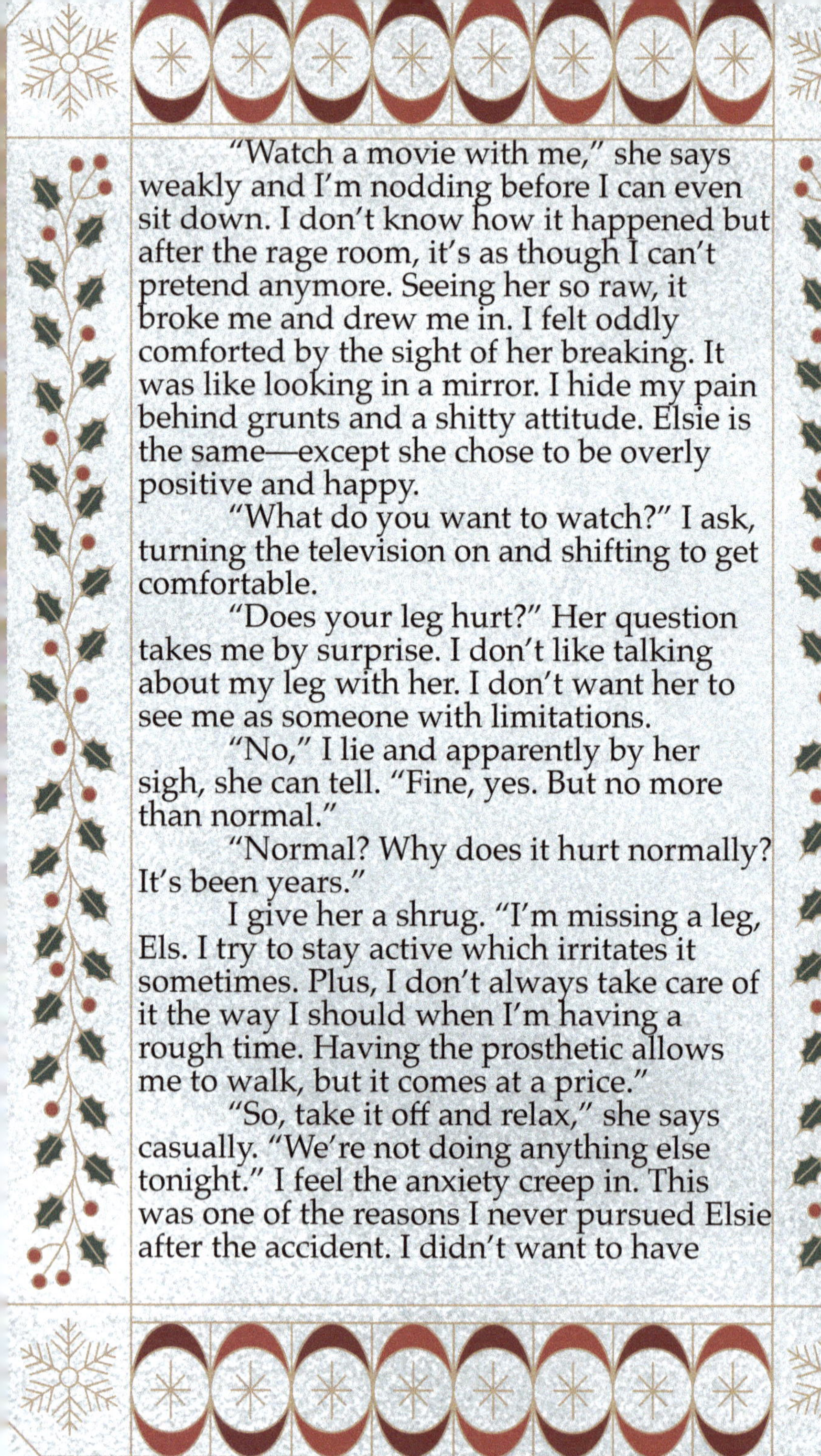

"Watch a movie with me," she says weakly and I'm nodding before I can even sit down. I don't know how it happened but after the rage room, it's as though I can't pretend anymore. Seeing her so raw, it broke me and drew me in. I felt oddly comforted by the sight of her breaking. It was like looking in a mirror. I hide my pain behind grunts and a shitty attitude. Elsie is the same—except she chose to be overly positive and happy.

"What do you want to watch?" I ask, turning the television on and shifting to get comfortable.

"Does your leg hurt?" Her question takes me by surprise. I don't like talking about my leg with her. I don't want her to see me as someone with limitations.

"No," I lie and apparently by her sigh, she can tell. "Fine, yes. But no more than normal."

"Normal? Why does it hurt normally? It's been years."

I give her a shrug. "I'm missing a leg, Els. I try to stay active which irritates it sometimes. Plus, I don't always take care of it the way I should when I'm having a rough time. Having the prosthetic allows me to walk, but it comes at a price."

"So, take it off and relax," she says casually. "We're not doing anything else tonight." I feel the anxiety creep in. This was one of the reasons I never pursued Elsie after the accident. I didn't want to have these difficult conversations and I don't want her to see me without the prosthetic.

"That's alright," I grunt while focusing on the television. "It's best I leave it on in case I need to do something or take Holly outside." I can see out of the corner of my eye she's staring at me.

"Grant, I've seen you without your prosthetic before, why are you acting so shy?" she says the words cautiously and I take a deep breath while trying to not snap at her. She has a right to ask, and if I want her in my life, I'm going to have to be open.

"I'm aware," I state slowly. "But you're sick, if you need something and the prosthetic is off, it's going to be swollen and twice as painful to put back on if you need me."

"I'm a grown woman, I don't *need* you to do anything. But if I did, I know you have crutches." She gestures to my pair of crutches leaning on the wall.

"I'd rather not," I mutter.

"Grant—"

"Are we watching a movie or not?" It comes out a little harsher than I mean and I instantly feel like a prick when I hear the cracking of her knuckles.

"Y-Yeah—"

"Stop," I interrupt her. I know she's about to put on her mask and I can't handle it. "I'm sorry. I'm just self conscious, alright?"

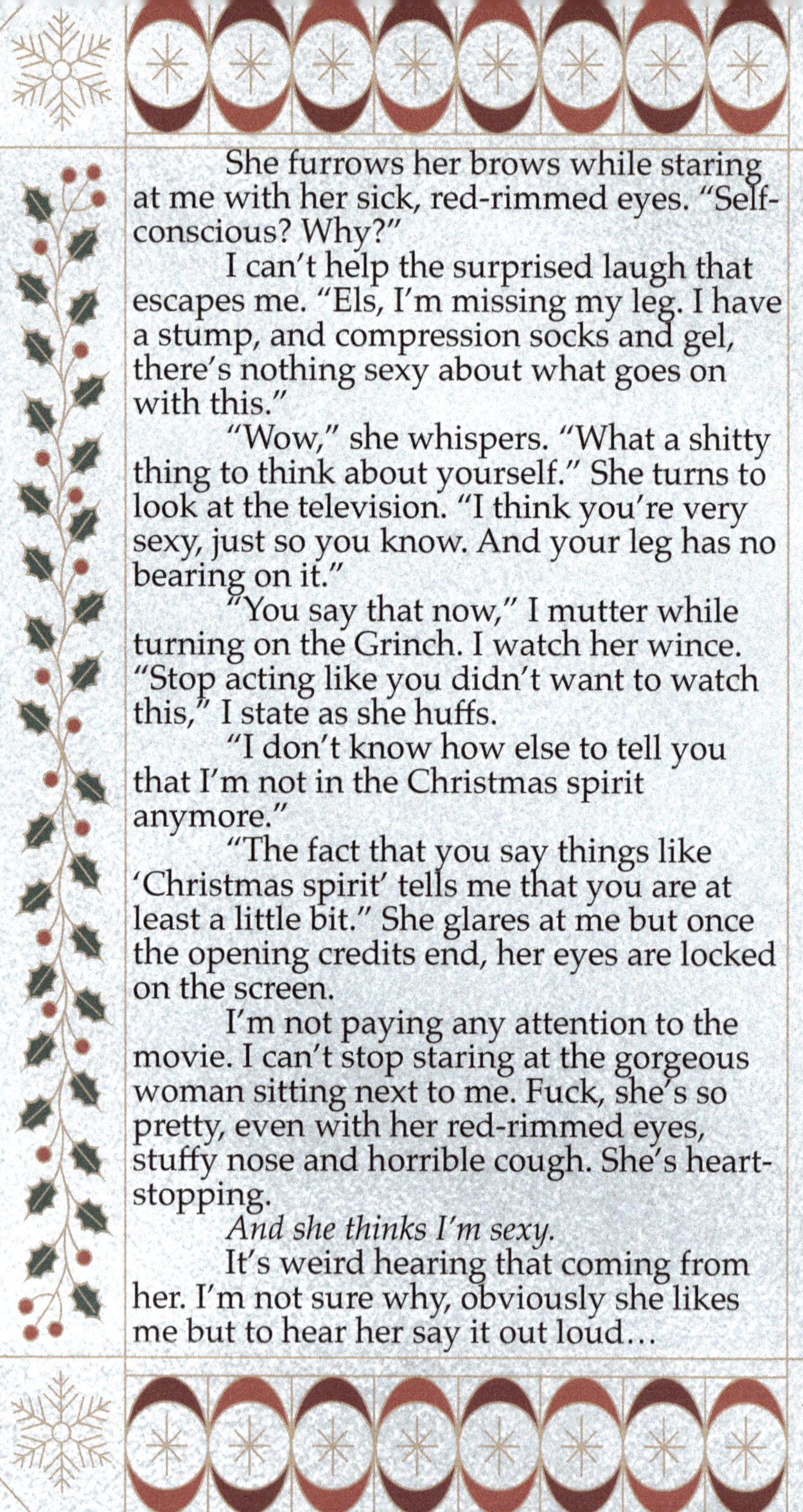

She furrows her brows while staring at me with her sick, red-rimmed eyes. "Self-conscious? Why?"

I can't help the surprised laugh that escapes me. "Els, I'm missing my leg. I have a stump, and compression socks and gel, there's nothing sexy about what goes on with this."

"Wow," she whispers. "What a shitty thing to think about yourself." She turns to look at the television. "I think you're very sexy, just so you know. And your leg has no bearing on it."

"You say that now," I mutter while turning on the Grinch. I watch her wince. "Stop acting like you didn't want to watch this," I state as she huffs.

"I don't know how else to tell you that I'm not in the Christmas spirit anymore."

"The fact that you say things like 'Christmas spirit' tells me that you are at least a little bit." She glares at me but once the opening credits end, her eyes are locked on the screen.

I'm not paying any attention to the movie. I can't stop staring at the gorgeous woman sitting next to me. Fuck, she's so pretty, even with her red-rimmed eyes, stuffy nose and horrible cough. She's heart-stopping.

And she thinks I'm sexy.

It's weird hearing that coming from her. I'm not sure why, obviously she likes me but to hear her say it out loud…

I run my hand over my jeans—
feeling the prosthetic and inwardly
groaning. She is the only one I've felt less-
than over this damn thing, and I don't
know why. Any other woman these past
years, it's been nothing to tell them and
move on. It was never a big deal. But for
her, for Elsie… What if she needs
something from me and this fucking thing
stops me? Like when I couldn't carry her
through the snow. I mean, I would've tried.
Fuck, I was more than willing to have this
thing snap and shatter while trying to carry
her. But she wouldn't let me. She wouldn't
let me and she deserves a man that doesn't
have these types of limitat—

My breath catches as Elsie's head
rests on my shoulder. She's asleep. She lets
out a small whimper and nuzzles into the
crook of my neck. I can't fight the small
smile forming as I grab her hand in mine. I
may have physical limitations, but my love
for Elsie—it's limitless and I think it's time I
show that to her.

12

ELSIE

"**O**uch!" I yelp while glaring at the offending espresso machine. Today is a bad day. I don't know what planet or star has shifted but everything that can go wrong, is going wrong.

I spilled milk on my shirt, I dropped a tray full of cups, Betty came in to the shop to remind me that I needed to work harder on the vendor set up because her top people were getting upset, and I dropped one of my contacts somewhere so I'm in my glasses which keep fogging up every time I use the steamer.

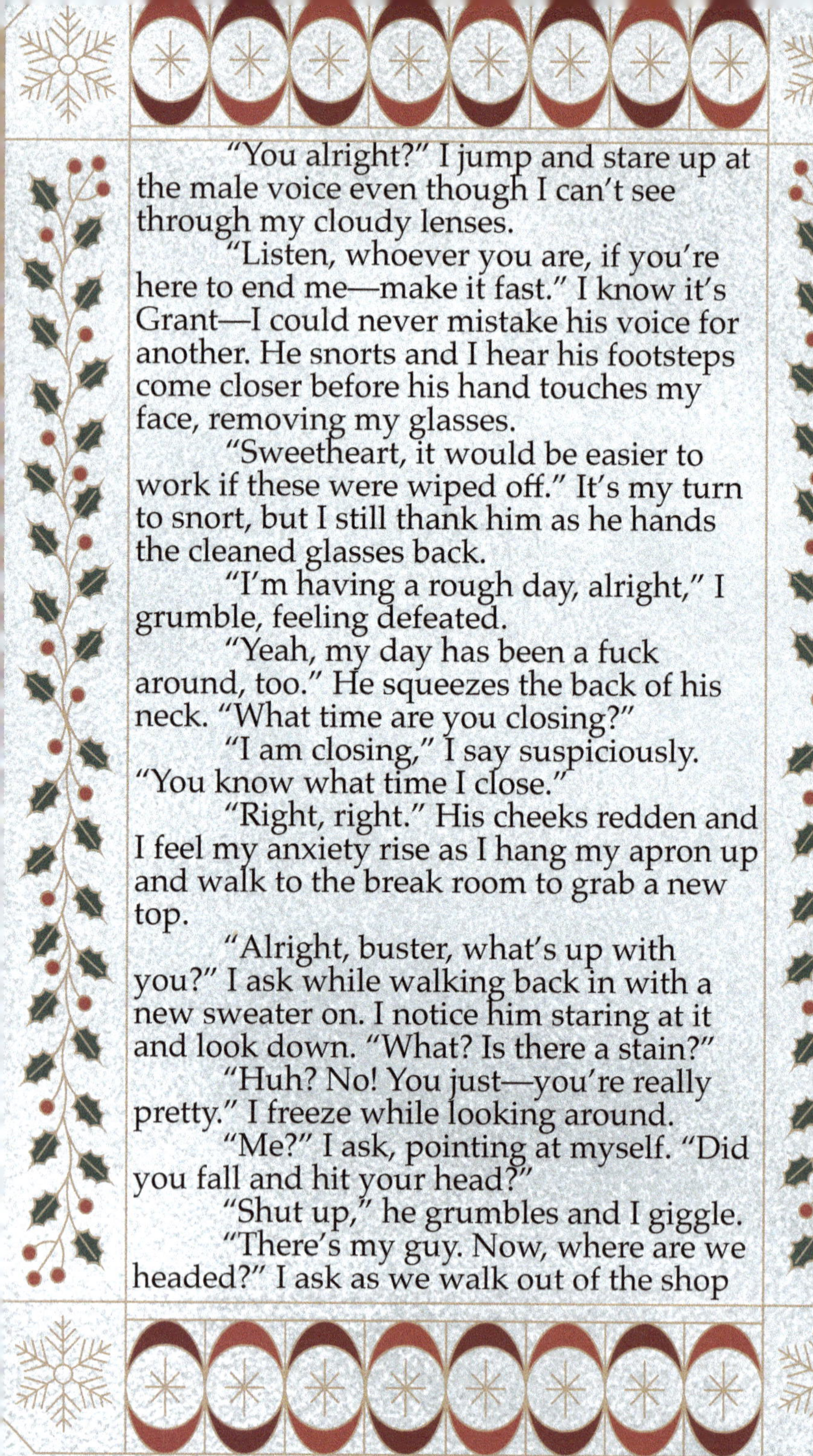

"You alright?" I jump and stare up at the male voice even though I can't see through my cloudy lenses.

"Listen, whoever you are, if you're here to end me—make it fast." I know it's Grant—I could never mistake his voice for another. He snorts and I hear his footsteps come closer before his hand touches my face, removing my glasses.

"Sweetheart, it would be easier to work if these were wiped off." It's my turn to snort, but I still thank him as he hands the cleaned glasses back.

"I'm having a rough day, alright," I grumble, feeling defeated.

"Yeah, my day has been a fuck around, too." He squeezes the back of his neck. "What time are you closing?"

"I am closing," I say suspiciously. "You know what time I close."

"Right, right." His cheeks redden and I feel my anxiety rise as I hang my apron up and walk to the break room to grab a new top.

"Alright, buster, what's up with you?" I ask while walking back in with a new sweater on. I notice him staring at it and look down. "What? Is there a stain?"

"Huh? No! You just—you're really pretty." I freeze while looking around.

"Me?" I ask, pointing at myself. "Did you fall and hit your head?"

"Shut up," he grumbles and I giggle.

"There's my guy. Now, where are we headed?" I ask as we walk out of the shop and lock the door. "Because if it's too far I'm going to need food…" I trail off as I stare at the large black pick-up that Grant is unlocking.

"Where's the other truck?" I force out, anxiety and dread filling me.

"My house," he grunts while sliding into the driver's seat. "I just bought her today." I tentatively climb into the cab and shut the door.

"It's really nice," I say softly while running my hand over the gray leather interior.

"Yeah, it's got all the bells and whistles, and I had them alter the pedals so they were easier for me to use."

"Oh, so you upgraded to make it easier! That makes sense! I'm happy for—"

"No," he interrupts while starting the ignition. "I bought the truck for you, so that you didn't feel panic when you got in a vehicle with me." My hands go to my aching chest as I stare at him, my eyes beginning to water.

"Are you serious? Me? You bought this just so I would be comfortable? Grant, we don't go that many places together."

"Yes, well, I'm working on changing that, first off. And second, I don't care if I'm in the truck with you everyday or once a year. Seeing that look on your face—even once, is too much. I won't let it happen if I can help it. And I can help this—what are you doing?" I ignore his question as I slide over the cab and straddle his lap.

"Am I hurting you?" I murmur and he shakes his head no. "Good." I lean in and capture his lips in mine.

"Fuck," he whimpers on a sharp exhale while tangling his hand in my hair, deepening the kiss. I moan against him as his tongue wraps around mine and my hands slide between us, landing on the crotch of his pants.

"Elsie," he breathes as my hand massages him through his pants. "Fuck!" he growls out, smacking the door as his head rolls back against the headrest. "F-Fuck, sweetheart—ah right… right there," he groans as I rub his hardening dick faster.

"Take your dick out," I pant out against his mouth. His pupils dilate as he fumbles to unbuckle his belt. As soon as his zipper is down I reach in and grip his dick with my hand.

"Oh, God!" His guttural moan is nearly my undoing. Leaning in, I lick the lobe of his ear before nipping at it.

"Mmmm… am I your God now, Grant?" I purr while stroking his… Oh my God…

Glancing down I see the holy shit erection and I try, I really do, but I know the shock is written all over my face. Grant's dick, it's massive. Like… what the actual fuck massive. I stare at him and he's so full of lust and pleasure that I'm not even sure he's on this planet anymore.

"Fuck me," I pant, causing his eyes to snap into focus.

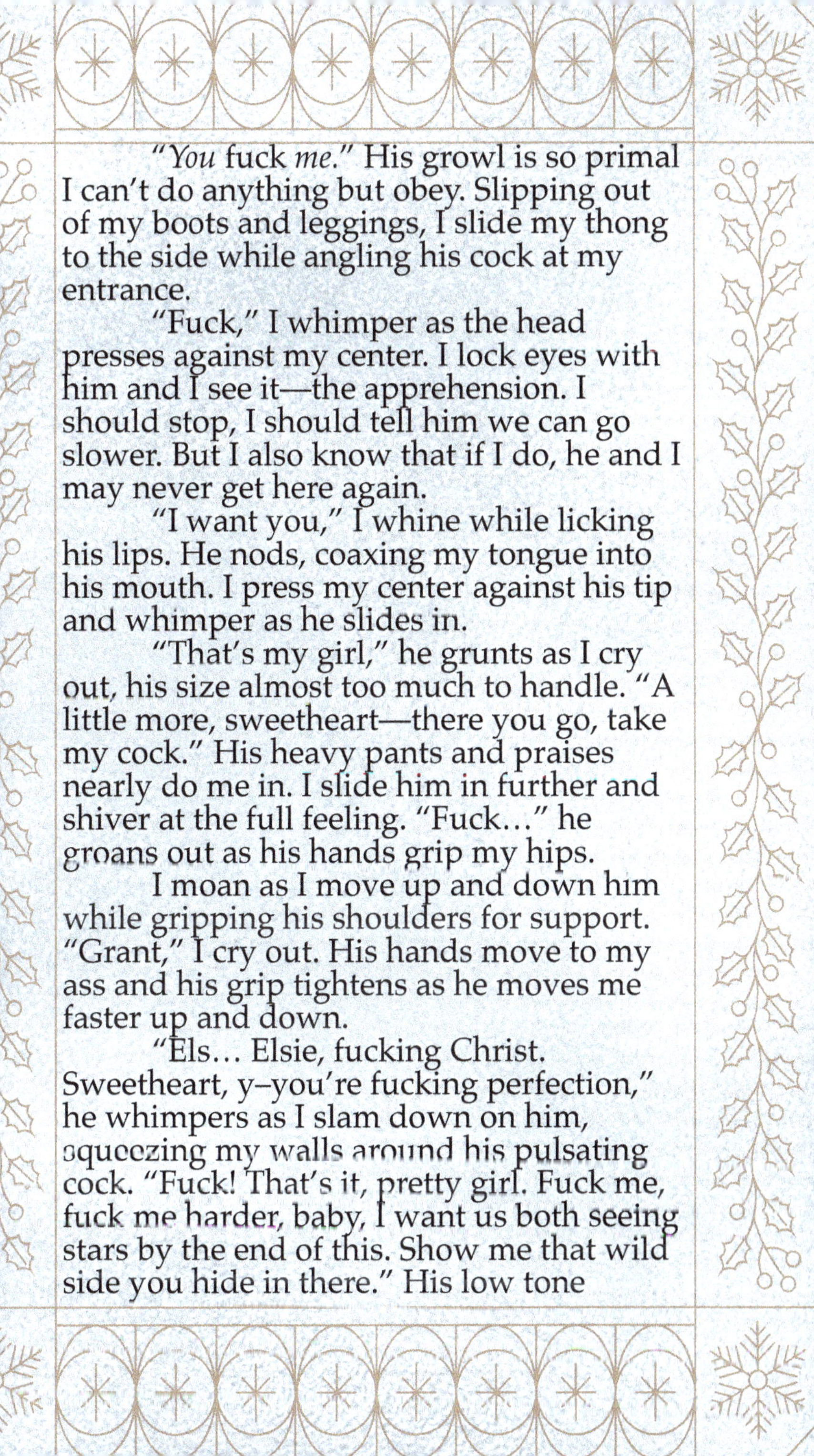

"*You* fuck *me*." His growl is so primal I can't do anything but obey. Slipping out of my boots and leggings, I slide my thong to the side while angling his cock at my entrance.

"Fuck," I whimper as the head presses against my center. I lock eyes with him and I see it—the apprehension. I should stop, I should tell him we can go slower. But I also know that if I do, he and I may never get here again.

"I want you," I whine while licking his lips. He nods, coaxing my tongue into his mouth. I press my center against his tip and whimper as he slides in.

"That's my girl," he grunts as I cry out, his size almost too much to handle. "A little more, sweetheart—there you go, take my cock." His heavy pants and praises nearly do me in. I slide him in further and shiver at the full feeling. "Fuck…" he groans out as his hands grip my hips.

I moan as I move up and down him while gripping his shoulders for support. "Grant," I cry out. His hands move to my ass and his grip tightens as he moves me faster up and down.

"Els… Elsie, fucking Christ. Sweetheart, y–you're fucking perfection," he whimpers as I slam down on him, squeezing my walls around his pulsating cock. "Fuck! That's it, pretty girl. Fuck me, fuck me harder, baby, I want us both seeing stars by the end of this. Show me that wild side you hide in there." His low tone

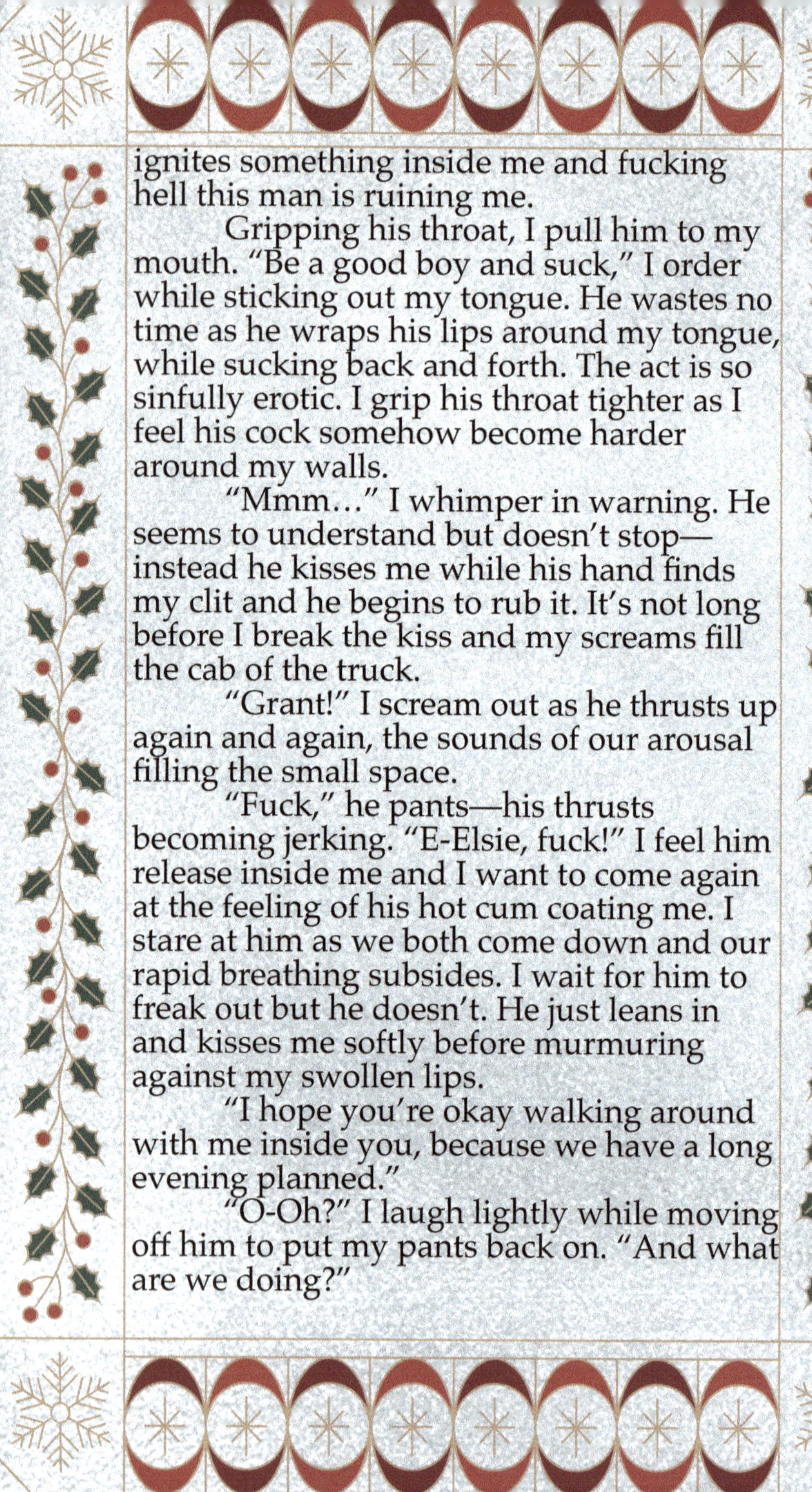

ignites something inside me and fucking hell this man is ruining me.

Gripping his throat, I pull him to my mouth. "Be a good boy and suck," I order while sticking out my tongue. He wastes no time as he wraps his lips around my tongue, while sucking back and forth. The act is so sinfully erotic. I grip his throat tighter as I feel his cock somehow become harder around my walls.

"Mmm…" I whimper in warning. He seems to understand but doesn't stop—instead he kisses me while his hand finds my clit and he begins to rub it. It's not long before I break the kiss and my screams fill the cab of the truck.

"Grant!" I scream out as he thrusts up again and again, the sounds of our arousal filling the small space.

"Fuck," he pants—his thrusts becoming jerking. "E-Elsie, fuck!" I feel him release inside me and I want to come again at the feeling of his hot cum coating me. I stare at him as we both come down and our rapid breathing subsides. I wait for him to freak out but he doesn't. He just leans in and kisses me softly before murmuring against my swollen lips.

"I hope you're okay walking around with me inside you, because we have a long evening planned."

"O-Oh?" I laugh lightly while moving off him to put my pants back on. "And what are we doing?"

"Gotta decorate headquarters, right?" I stop just as I'm about to tug my leggings over my butt to stare at him.

"Headquarters?" He can't be saying what I think he is… can he?

Grant gives me a shy smile. "You said my house is headquarters for Project Chestnuts, so I thought we'd go get the stuff to decorate." I can't fight the smile forming on my face.

"Really? You mean I get to decorate your house? Really?"

"Living Room and front porch. That's what I'm willing to give up this year."

"Oh my God! This is the best surprise ever!" I squeal as Grant snorts while putting his truck into drive.

"I bought a new truck for you and we just fucked but Christmas shopping is the best part of the night?" I give him a cheeky smile before leaning in and kissing his cheek.

"I know how hard all of this is, thank you for doing it."

"It's hard, yeah, but I would do anything to keep you smiling at me like that, now let's go."

13

GRANT

I told Elsie just my living room and the front porch would be decorated for Christmas this year. What I failed was giving her a limit on the decorations she could put in those two areas. I look from the twinkling Christmas tree that fucking spins to my dog. Not even poor Holly was safe from the decorations. Our eyes meet, and fuck, she looks like such a goofball with those antlers on. But she's letting Elsie do it, which seems to only delight Elsie more.

All I'm saying is it's a good fucking thing she fucked my brains out because otherwise I would've went into asshole mode ten minutes after she started loading the buggy. Fuck, that girl will be the end of me. She slipped my cock inside her and it was over. I wanted to weep while I worshiped her. She's perfection—beyond perfection. The way we connected, like we were made for each other. It was too much, I nearly came at the start.

"Grant." She beams, and fucking God I'm a goner.

"Yeah, sweetheart?" I look at the contents in her hand and scowl. "Oh, fuck no. I told you at the store I'm not doing it." She holds the garments to her chest while pushing out her bottom lip.

"Okay," she pouts. "I'll just wear it all by my—"

"Give me the damn thing," I grumble while snatching the black shirt and red plaid pants. "One time—don't think you can whip that lip out and get your way whenever you see fit," I huff while poking her lip into her mouth before heading to my room to change.

"Well," Elsie hums while following behind me. "I could just suck your dick if pouting doesn't work." The clothes fall from my hand, landing on the floor as I stare at her in shock.

"You know," I cough while trying to regain my composure. "For such a sweet girl, you sure do have a filthy mouth." Elsie stalks up to me, a sly smile on her pretty face.

"If you think that's filthy." She grabs my neck, pulling me down to her face as her

hand goes over her head. "Imagine the things I don't say." I glance up at the mistletoe she's holding above us and smirk.

"Hmmm…" Standing straight, I hold her wrist and lower the mistletoe, past her breasts, her stomach, and landing right above her pussy. "Would ya look at that." I grin while walking us to the bed so I can sit on the edge.

"You wouldn't." She gasps as I pull her hips to me, pressing my lips against the front of her pants-covered pussy.

"I take mistletoe rules *very* seriously," I murmur while nuzzling into her mound. She pulls back while raising a brow.

"How seriously?" she asks and—*holy fuck, there goes her pants and underwear.* Her shirt and bra are next, leaving her completely naked. Her soft hips are begging to be gripped. Her large tits… Fuck, I need to taste them and that glistening pussy…

She wiggles the mistletoe above her bare pussy again and I feel the growl escape me as I scoot back on the bed. "Come here," I order while removing my shirt. Elsie obeys, crawling across my bed. Feeling impatient, I grip her and pull her so she's straddling my face.

"Grant!" she cries out and I feel her about to move off. Fuck that. Gripping her hip, I lock her into place and grab her arm with my free hand. I place her hand—still holding the mistletoe—above her pussy.

"Don't you fucking move it," I warn while tightening my grip on her hip as I drag my tongue over her wet pussy.

"Holy shit—"

"Don't move it!" I growl over her gasp as she tries to drop the mistletoe. I see her grip tighten as I lick again. "That's my girl. You ready to suffocate me?" I nuzzle into her, pulling her clit into my mouth and giving it a suck.

"Ah! G-Grant, yes!" she cries as her head falls back.

"Ride my face, Elsie, I want to consume you. Don't you let air or daylight between us." I smirk at her cry as I slip my tongue into her wet center and lap her up. I feel her hips buck, she's timid at first, but soon we find a rhythm and she's gripping my headboard with one hand while holding the mistletoe with the other.

"Right there," she whines as her hips move in a circle. I capture her clit between my lips—giving it a rough suck before teasing her with my tongue. Her thighs are shaking as I grab her ass in my hands and pull her further on me while plunging my tongue inside her and nuzzling her clit with my nose.

"Grant!" she screams as she bucks erratically—her body spasming as she rides out her orgasm. I lap her up completely and when she's too sensitive, I allow her to move. She slips off me and takes a seat on the edge of the bed.

"What are you thinking?" I ask while kissing her shoulder.

"That this is going to hurt when it's over." Her blunt statement takes me by surprise. I sit up and slide to the edge of the bed beside her.

"Sweetheart, why do you think this is going to end?"

"Two weeks ago you barely would give me more than a grunt. Now you bought a truck, we've had sex, and we've never even been on a date. I told you I have feelings for you, but you—"

"Els," I breathe out while running a hand through my hair. "Everything you're saying is fair." I watch as she stands to put on her pajamas. "I was going to ask you to go ice skating," I admit, despite the dread growing in my gut. Elsie pulls her shirt down and grabs her glasses—putting them back on.

"What?" Her brows furrow behind her dark frames. She's so fucking cute.

"The night I wrecked, I had talked to David while we were at work. I was going to ask you out the following day." Her mouth drops as she sits back on the bed.

"Really?" she breathes in disbelief. "Me? Why?" I roll my eyes at her ridiculous question.

"Why? Els, baby, come on. I have been your shadow since we were kids. Even after the accident, it's obvious I couldn't leave you alone. I mean I go to the coffee shop twice a day, and I hate coffee."

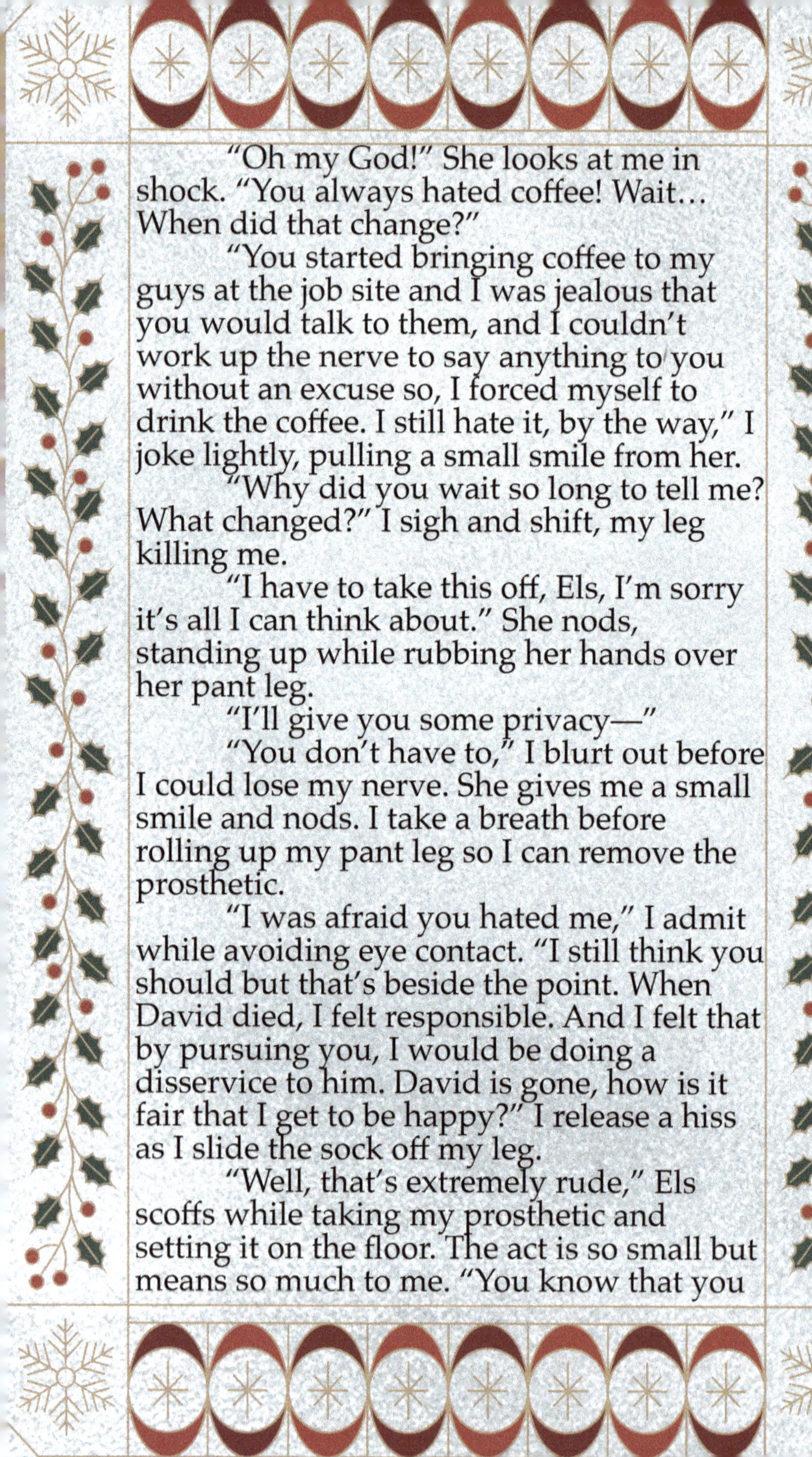

"Oh my God!" She looks at me in shock. "You always hated coffee! Wait… When did that change?"

"You started bringing coffee to my guys at the job site and I was jealous that you would talk to them, and I couldn't work up the nerve to say anything to you without an excuse so, I forced myself to drink the coffee. I still hate it, by the way," I joke lightly, pulling a small smile from her.

"Why did you wait so long to tell me? What changed?" I sigh and shift, my leg killing me.

"I have to take this off, Els, I'm sorry it's all I can think about." She nods, standing up while rubbing her hands over her pant leg.

"I'll give you some privacy—"

"You don't have to," I blurt out before I could lose my nerve. She gives me a small smile and nods. I take a breath before rolling up my pant leg so I can remove the prosthetic.

"I was afraid you hated me," I admit while avoiding eye contact. "I still think you should but that's beside the point. When David died, I felt responsible. And I felt that by pursuing you, I would be doing a disservice to him. David is gone, how is it fair that I get to be happy?" I release a hiss as I slide the sock off my leg.

"Well, that's extremely rude," Els scoffs while taking my prosthetic and setting it on the floor. The act is so small but means so much to me. "You know that you can't use my brother as an excuse forever, right? It's unfair to his memory and we both know that if he were alive today he'd kick your ass for that."

"It's not meant as an excuse," I grunt out. This conversation is more than just a little uncomfortable. "But how is it fair?"

"How is it fair to use his memory that way?" Her question gives me pause. I look at her as she pushes her glasses up the bridge of her nose.

"I—I guess it's not," I whisper softly as she crawls across the bed to cuddle against me.

"This will take time and work." She presses her lips to my shoulder as our hands intertwine. "But if you're willing to work at it, I am too. We'll just take it slow and be as honest as possible."

"It's not going to be easy," I warn her as she giggles.
"Well, that'll just make things spicy."

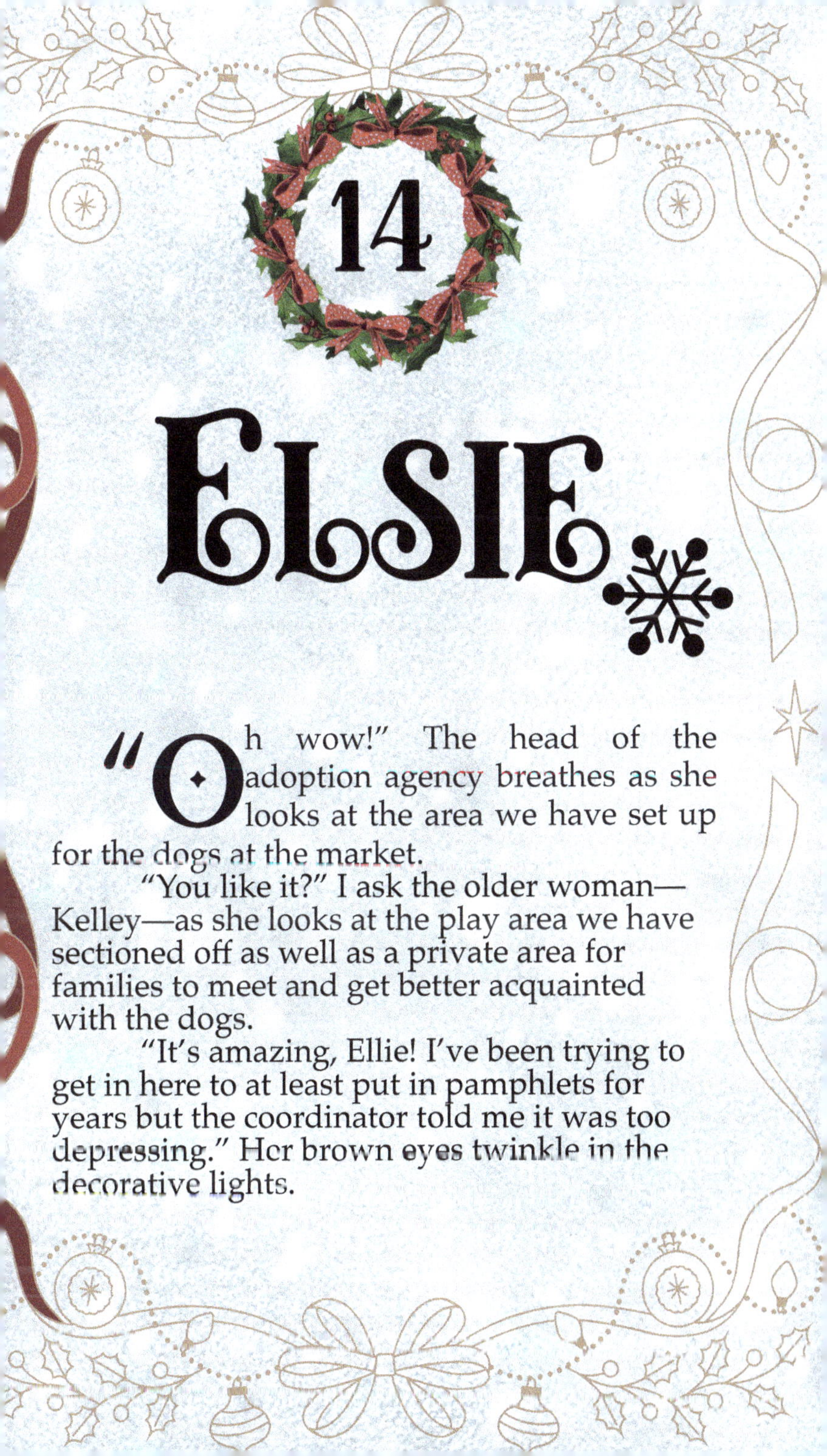

14

ELSIE

"Oh wow!" The head of the adoption agency breathes as she looks at the area we have set up for the dogs at the market.

"You like it?" I ask the older woman—Kelley—as she looks at the play area we have sectioned off as well as a private area for families to meet and get better acquainted with the dogs.

"It's amazing, Ellie! I've been trying to get in here to at least put in pamphlets for years but the coordinator told me it was too depressing." Her brown eyes twinkle in the decorative lights.

"Yes, well, I may only be in charge this year, but I am going to do the most with the power I have." Before Betty publicly executes me, that is. It's vendor set-up day and to say I've made enemies over this would be an understatement. Betty's friends are angry, and several have boycotted the marketplace due to my not giving them first spots. I instead gave it to the Santa workshop, the dog rescue we got Holly from and several other charitable vendors. There's even a booth for a children's hospital project where the people dress up like princess characters. I also added a giving tree and remembrance tree where you can make and add an ornament for loved ones who have passed. I wanted to have exciting and engaging, yet important things at the front of the marketplace to remind everyone what Christmas is about. It's not the gifts, the shopping or the rush, it's about love. It's about finding joy in something and trying to spread that joy to another soul. And that's who fills the first booths—vendors who spread joy.

I jump as a pair of strong arms wrap around my waist. I smile softly while looking up at Grant. He's so beautiful, and I'm so lucky that I've been able to work with him to chip away at his walls. It's going to take a lot of work on both our parts. He and I have years of guilt we've buried and it's not going to go away just like that. But I know that with everything we've been through, we can get through this, too. I never thought I would get to have my time with Grant, to have him as mine. It's… Well, without sounding cheesy, it's nothing short of a Christmas miracle and I'm so thankful for it and for him.

"You did a great job, Sweetheart," he murmurs while kissing my cheek. I blush and giggle lightly while turning in his arms to meet his gaze.

"I couldn't have done it without you." Looking up I smile softly at the mistletoe hanging over us and give him a small smile. "I mean, it's the rule," I say as he smirks.

"Yeah, we can't break that rule. I told you, I take mistletoe *very* seriously," he murmurs before pressing his lips to mine and holding me as I melt into his kiss.

I've been given the greatest gift. Not the marketplace, not even Grant as my boyfriend. But I've gotten to see Grant open himself up, I've seen him allow others in and I've watched his smile return and I'll forever be grateful for everything that's happened this season to get us to this moment, right here, together.

GRANT

Opening my eyes, I have to hold back a scream of surprise when I'm met with Elsie's face, an inch from mine.

"Jesus, Els, can I help you?" She giggles while situating herself on my stomach. *Hmmm that's it, sweetheart, wiggle that ass a little further south and we're gonna start this morning off right.*

"Merry Christmas!" She beams before placing a quick kiss on the tip of my nose. I give her a small chuckle as I grab her softly by the back of the neck and pull her to me, giving her a proper kiss. I groan against her mouth as her center grinds over me.

"Keep that up, sweetheart and you won't leave this bed until New Years." She giggles before pushing me back on the bed.

"Nice try, buddy, you aren't getting sex until I get my present." I groan in protest while giving her a playful smack on her ass as she gets up.

"It's Christmas, I should be allowed to receive a little cheer," I mumble while grabbing my crutches and following her and Holly to the living room. It's completely decorated—like the rest of the house—in Christmas decorations. I smell the hot chocolate on the stove, and the sound of a Christmas movie playing fills my ears.

"How long have you been up?" I laugh lightly as Elsie shrugs.

"A couple hours, I wanted to handle some last minute things before our trip." Elsie's gift to me is a vacation to the beach. At first I was apprehensive, I haven't traveled since my accident and I'm unsure how I'm going to handle the sand. But, after discussing it with her and my therapist, I realized it's just fear of the unknown, and that shouldn't stop me from enjoying my life with the woman I love.

"There are so many presents with my name!" Elsie gasps before glaring at me. "You promised not to go crazy." I sit on the couch before shrugging.

"I seem to remember you telling me not to buy you too much and I said that I'll buy you what I want and you can deal with it."

She giggles before tossing me a wrapped box and reaching in a stocking to

pull out an elk antler for Holly who excitedly takes it before trotting off. I open the box and can't help the smile as I lift the garment.

"Think it'll fit me?" I tease, holding the green bra to my chest. "Oh, a thong and… candy cane stockings? Els, I don't know, what if the townspeople find out—ow!" I laugh as she smacks my arm before straddling my lap.

"Keep talking, Grant," she purrs in my ear. "And you won't end up on the naughty list."

"Oh, now we can't have that," I murmur into her neck while reaching behind the pillow on the couch and holding up a spiky, round object between us.

"What's that?" She laughs while poking one of the spikes.

"Horse Chestnut shell," I say casually even though on the inside I'm sweaty and nauseous.

"Oh my God! Operation Chestnuts!" she squeals through her laughter.

"Yeah," I say nervously. "I thought maybe it was time to bring it back, ya know, for one more operation?" Her brow raises above the rim of her glasses as she cocks her head to one side.

"You know after the madness last year that I hung my elf hat up for good." I do know that. Despite the massive success of the Christmas Marketplace, Els chose not to return this year, giving the job to Kelley, the adoption coordinator. Shocking to no

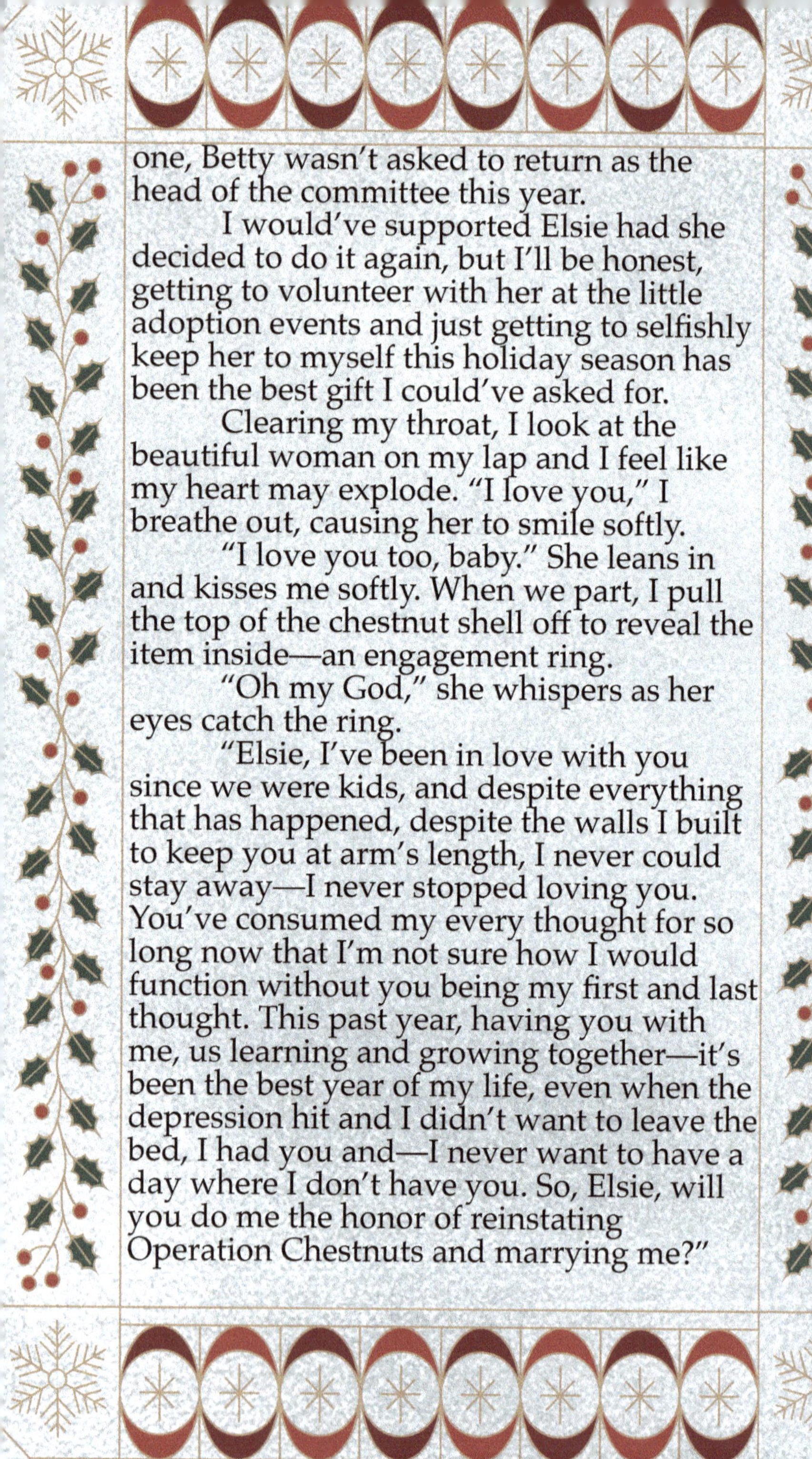

one, Betty wasn't asked to return as the head of the committee this year.

I would've supported Elsie had she decided to do it again, but I'll be honest, getting to volunteer with her at the little adoption events and just getting to selfishly keep her to myself this holiday season has been the best gift I could've asked for.

Clearing my throat, I look at the beautiful woman on my lap and I feel like my heart may explode. "I love you," I breathe out, causing her to smile softly.

"I love you too, baby." She leans in and kisses me softly. When we part, I pull the top of the chestnut shell off to reveal the item inside—an engagement ring.

"Oh my God," she whispers as her eyes catch the ring.

"Elsie, I've been in love with you since we were kids, and despite everything that has happened, despite the walls I built to keep you at arm's length, I never could stay away—I never stopped loving you. You've consumed my every thought for so long now that I'm not sure how I would function without you being my first and last thought. This past year, having you with me, us learning and growing together—it's been the best year of my life, even when the depression hit and I didn't want to leave the bed, I had you and—I never want to have a day where I don't have you. So, Elsie, will you do me the honor of reinstating Operation Chestnuts and marrying me?"

She giggles and tears spill from her cheeks as she nods frantically.

"Yes! I will!"

"Oh, thank god!" I breathe out a laugh as I pull her to me, pressing her lips to mine. "I love you," I whisper over and over again.

"I love you, too."

"Is that too tight?" I ask while tugging on the colorful strand of lights. Elsie shakes her head as her bound arms raise with the tug. I marvel at my girl—my fiancée. She's on her knees in that sexy thong and bra which pushes her tits up in the most fantastic way. Her candy cane thigh high socks are so god damn hot I nearly came at the sight of them.

"Wow," she breathes, her eyes zeroing in on my crotch. "I wonder if I'll ever not be shocked at how big you are." I chuckle while stepping toward her. Her peachy mouth opens almost on instinct and her sweet tongue slips out.

"You want something, my beautiful wife-to-be?" She leans forward but my hold on the light stand holds her steady. "Use your words."

"Grant," she whimpers—her breasts swelling with each ragged breath. "I want you to ram your cock down my throat, make me cry, tug my hair as you thrust down my throat until I'm choking on you

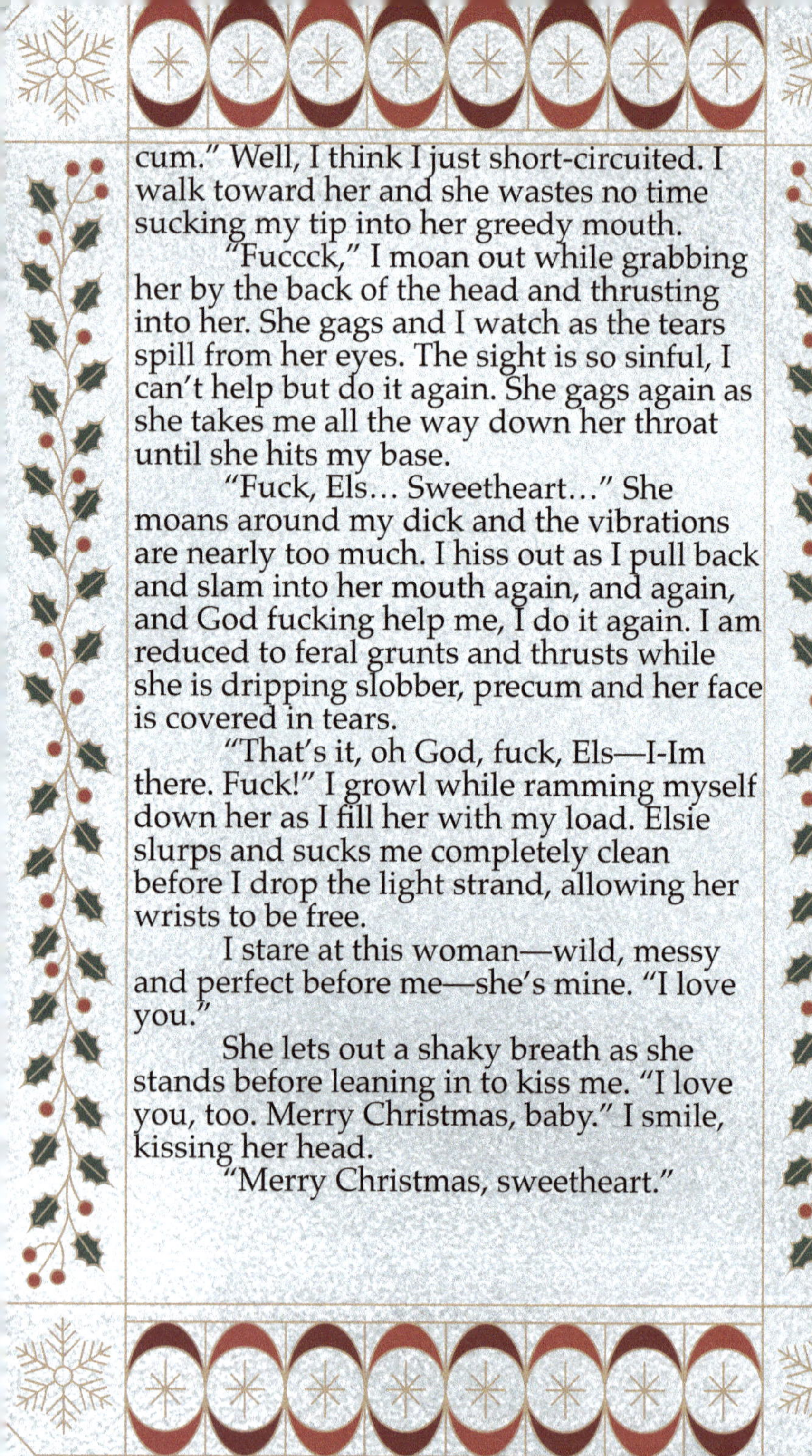

cum." Well, I think I just short-circuited. I walk toward her and she wastes no time sucking my tip into her greedy mouth.

"Fuccck," I moan out while grabbing her by the back of the head and thrusting into her. She gags and I watch as the tears spill from her eyes. The sight is so sinful, I can't help but do it again. She gags again as she takes me all the way down her throat until she hits my base.

"Fuck, Els… Sweetheart…" She moans around my dick and the vibrations are nearly too much. I hiss out as I pull back and slam into her mouth again, and again, and God fucking help me, I do it again. I am reduced to feral grunts and thrusts while she is dripping slobber, precum and her face is covered in tears.

"That's it, oh God, fuck, Els—I-Im there. Fuck!" I growl while ramming myself down her as I fill her with my load. Elsie slurps and sucks me completely clean before I drop the light strand, allowing her wrists to be free.

I stare at this woman—wild, messy and perfect before me—she's mine. "I love you."

She lets out a shaky breath as she stands before leaning in to kiss me. "I love you, too. Merry Christmas, baby." I smile, kissing her head.

"Merry Christmas, sweetheart."

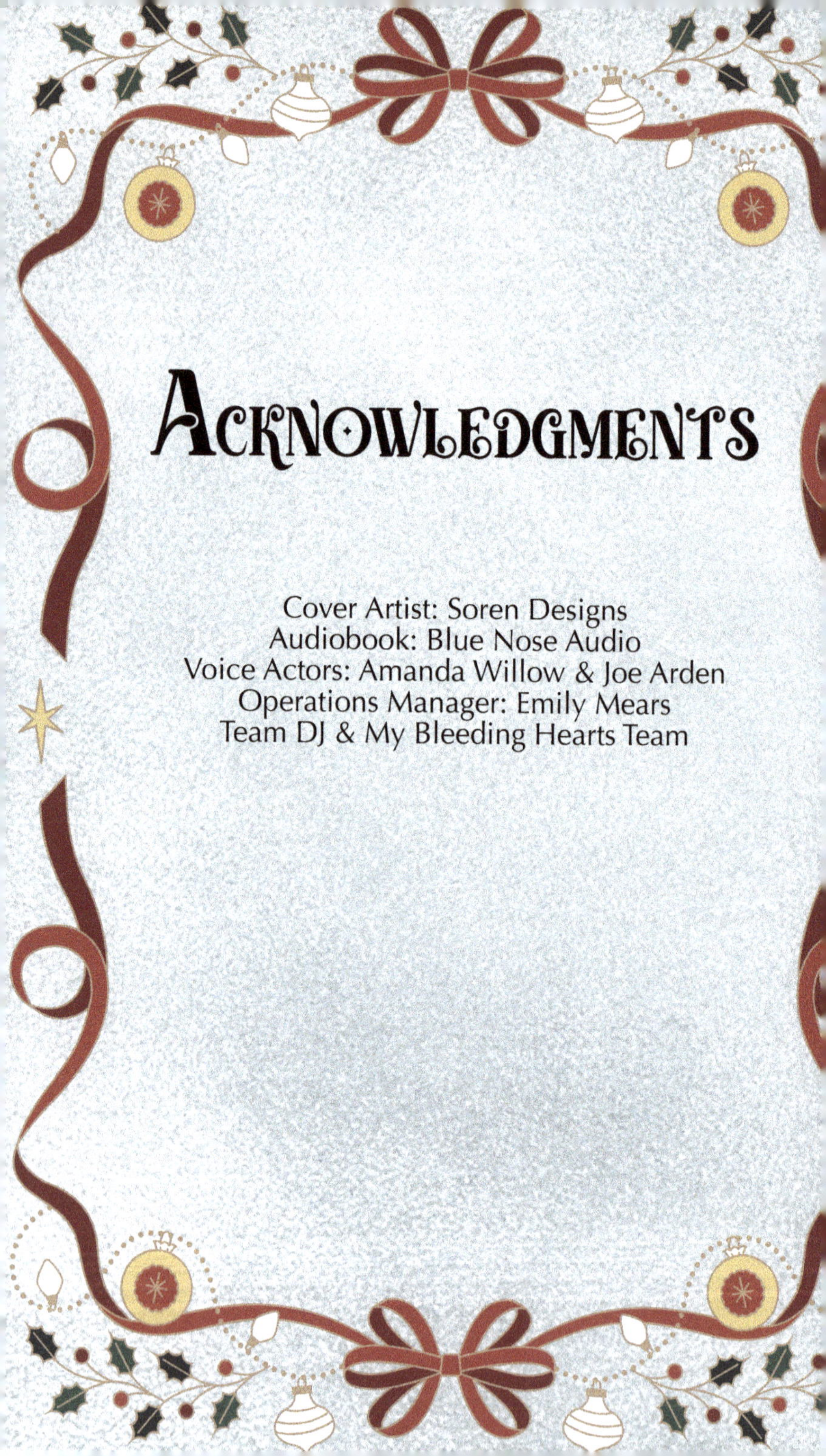

Acknowledgments

Cover Artist: Soren Designs
Audiobook: Blue Nose Audio
Voice Actors: Amanda Willow & Joe Arden
Operations Manager: Emily Mears
Team DJ & My Bleeding Hearts Team

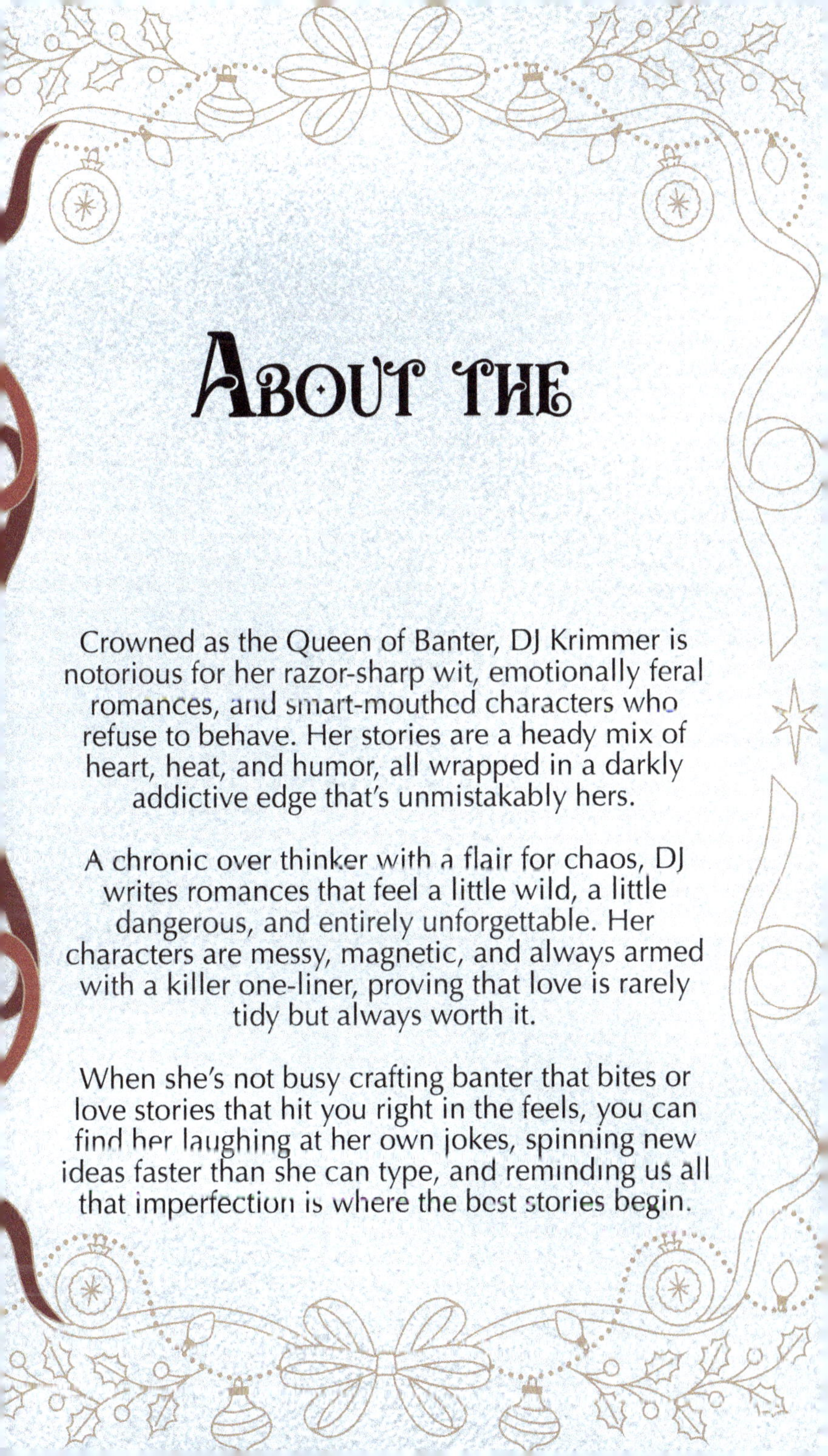

About the

Crowned as the Queen of Banter, DJ Krimmer is notorious for her razor-sharp wit, emotionally feral romances, and smart-mouthed characters who refuse to behave. Her stories are a heady mix of heart, heat, and humor, all wrapped in a darkly addictive edge that's unmistakably hers.

A chronic over thinker with a flair for chaos, DJ writes romances that feel a little wild, a little dangerous, and entirely unforgettable. Her characters are messy, magnetic, and always armed with a killer one-liner, proving that love is rarely tidy but always worth it.

When she's not busy crafting banter that bites or love stories that hit you right in the feels, you can find her laughing at her own jokes, spinning new ideas faster than she can type, and reminding us all that imperfection is where the best stories begin.

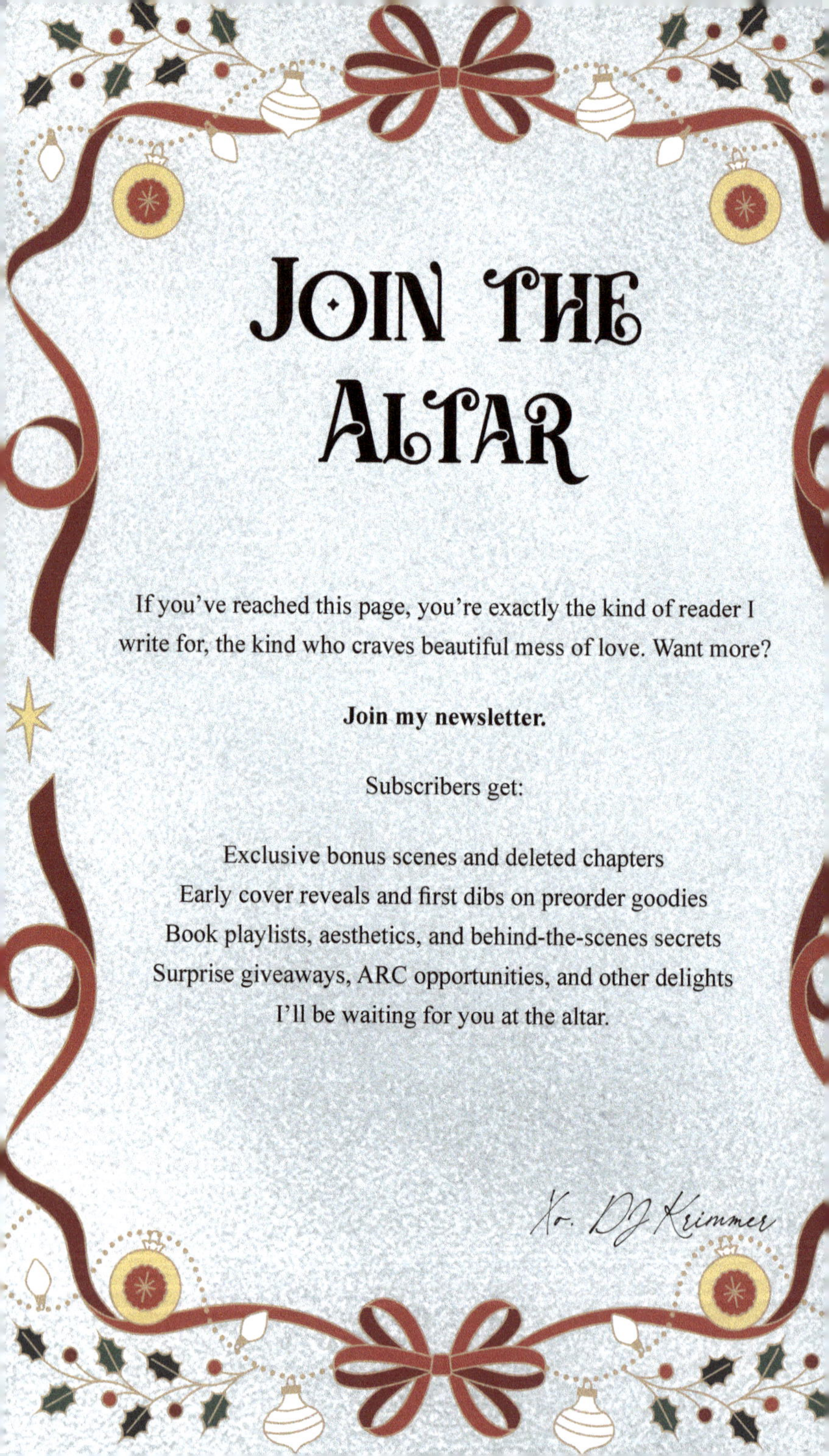

JOIN THE ALTAR

If you've reached this page, you're exactly the kind of reader I write for, the kind who craves beautiful mess of love. Want more?

Join my newsletter.

Subscribers get:

Exclusive bonus scenes and deleted chapters
Early cover reveals and first dibs on preorder goodies
Book playlists, aesthetics, and behind-the-scenes secrets
Surprise giveaways, ARC opportunities, and other delights
I'll be waiting for you at the altar.

Xo. DJ Krimmer

COME STALK

Website - djkrimmer.com
Facebook - facebook.com/groups/djkrimmer
Tiktok - @authordjkrimmer
Instagram - @djkrimmer

9 798330 638659